PULP Literature

Pulp Literature Press

Issue No. 34, Spring 2022

Publisher: Pulp Literature Press; Managing Editor: Jennifer Landels; Senior Editor: Mel Anastasiou; Acquisitions Editor: Genevieve Wynand; Poetry Editors: Daniel Cowper & Emily Osborne; Assistant Editors: Samantha Olson, Brooklynn Hook, Veronika Kos, Melisa Gruger; Copy Editor: Amanda Bidnall; Proofreader: Mary Rykov; Graphic Design: Amanda Bidnall; Cover Design: Kate Landels; First Readers: Carol McCauley, Brenda Carre, Jeya Thiessen; Subscriptions: Carol McCauley; Advertising: Brooklynn Hook. For advertising rates, direct inquiries to info@pulpliterature.com.

Cover painting, *Black Tortoise Kowtows* by Herman Lau. Obelisk image in 'Gumdrop: A Bekker Story' by JJ Lee. Cartoons by Hurricane Nancy. All other illustrations by Mel Anastasiou.

Pulp Literature: ISSN 2292-2164 (Print), ISSN 2292-2172 (Digital), Issue No. 34, Spring 2022.

Published quarterly by Pulp Literature Press, 21955 16 Ave, Langley, BC, Canada V2Z 1K5, pulpliterature.com, at $15.00 per copy. Annual subscription $50.00 in Canada, $72.00 in continental USA, $86.00 elsewhere. Printed in Victoria, BC, Canada, by First Choice Books / Victoria Bindery. Copyright © 2022 Pulp Literature Press. All stories and works of art copyright © 2022 their authors as per bylines.

Pulp Literature Press gratefully acknowledges the support of the Canada Council for the Arts.

Pulp Literature is a proud member of the Magazine Association of BC and Magazines Canada.

TABLE OF CONTENTS

FROM THE PULP LIT PULPIT

Have Space, Will Travel

There's a running joke here in south-western British Columbia. How many seasons are there in the Lower Mainland? Two: winter—and roadwork. Roadwork season begins when there's still enough frost on the grass and snap in the air to make you remember your gloves, but just enough warmth to abandon those gloves for about an hour each day at noon. Popping up everywhere like so many brave crocuses, flaggers are flagging, diggers are digging, levellers are levelling, and pavers are paving. And most of their attention is turned to filling in the umpteen potholes with which winter scarred the city streets.

The original potholes are circles; the filled-in patches are squares. To make the road whole again, the crew excises just enough space to make for an easier repair. And while those early-morning road crews are busy squaring their circles, you can find me hunched over my coffee and crosswords, trying to circle so many puzzling squares. Will Shortz, the long-time *New York Times* crossword puzzle editor, believes that when people see an empty square, they long to fill it. Surely, too, when a writer sees a blank page, they feel the urge to fill it. I've stared down enough blank pages and driven over enough of my own literary potholes to know this to be true.

The seeds of my writing life were planted early. Books and reading—and the spaces of reading—are giants of my childhood memories. Visiting the children's section of our local library, with

its alphabet carpet, tiered steps for storytime, kid-height shelves and orderly books. (You could spot the Blumes from the Clearys an LMNOP carpet-row away!) Standing still and quiet with my fellow kindergarten-soldiers in the hallway of our elementary school, waiting for the school librarian to open the doors to the land of lending cards and limitless wonder. Sitting in the back seat of the family station wagon as we barrelled through the Rockies, me paying more attention to my mountain of books than, well, the mountains of rock. I saw spaces in which to read, and I most definitely filled them.

To me, spring is the most spacious of seasons. It is the promise of the new, yes, but it is also the season in which things begin again to take up space. Animals away from hibernation. Buds away from branches. And we humans, hopefully, toward each other.

So, whether you are a city engineer filling yet another pothole, a writer fixing yet another plot-hole, or a young-at-heart reader who still craves books to feel whole, we salute you.

~*Genevieve Wynand*

In this issue Find strength in humility (and mud) with *Black Tortoise Kowtows* by cover artist **Herman Lau**. And journey to the ends of the earth — and the edge of reality — in 'Gumdrop: A Bekker Story' by feature author **JJ Lee**.

Time ticks ever forward in 'The Realm of Shadows' by **Megan W Shaw**, 'Pretty Lies: Fly Away' by **Mel Anastasiou**, and 'Would We Had Time' by **Lorina Stephens**.

Hannah van Didden with 'Gerald Bantam Says Goodbye', **Douglas Smith** with 'The Balance', and **Laura Kuhlmann** with 'A Jar of Marmalade' usher us to the other side of grief.

Pivot the moment with 'Clothesline' by **Kimberley Aslett** and 'Respawn' by **Michelle Barker**. And pivot the argument with 'A Gentleman's Primer' by **Mitchell Shanklin** and 'The Shepherdess: Artifice' by **JM Landels**.

Poetry by **Mitchell Bodo, Alex Kitt**, and **Derek Webster** asks life's big questions. And cartoons by **Hurricane Nancy** answer yes, it'll be all right.

GUMDROP: A BEKKER STORY

JJ Lee

JJ Lee wrote the memoir The Measure of a Man: The Story of a Father, a Son, and a Suit. *His monster-chaser Bekker has appeared in* Pulp Literature *twice before, in issues 8 and 24. JJ writes and records a Christmas ghost story for broadcast every year for CBC Radio, one of which we published in Issue 17, Winter 2018. In addition to the pen and ink drawings that accompany his stories, JJ has provided us with two cover paintings: 'Fallen Angel' based on Robert J Sawyer's story in Issue 7, and the iconic killer teddy bears of* Pulp Literature *Issue 2, featuring his story 'Built to Love'.*

Gumdrop: A Bekker Story

"The universal aptitude for ineptitude makes any human
accomplishment an incredible miracle."
~ *Dr John P Stapp, Project Manhigh*

I.

I borrowed a delivery bike from YC Sun, the grocer, without
asking. Why bother? I planned to bring it back before morning
and there would be no wear and tear. I only needed it as a prop,
and besides, riding it up Pacific Heights would have made me
cough up a lung.

I hoisted it onto my shoulder and hung from the rear runner
of the Jackson streetcar. I tried not to get chain grease on my
black button-down shirt or my strides. I'd just had Hong Tailors
make the pants, four pleats with a dropped belt-line, wide in
the thigh and narrow at the cuff. I took the streetcar to Sutter
and Gough, but I still had to push the bike two blocks to get
to Octavia and Washington. The hundred-foot climb may as
well have been the Swiss Alps. Though it was a cool summer

evening with a nice ocean breeze, by the time I reached Colonel Hobbs's house I was sweating bullets.

The street was lined with new Fords, Lincolns, Buicks, and Cadillacs — some as long as Sherman tanks — that gleamed in the setting sun. The mansionette on the corner was a Romanesque affair with rounded arches, three floors plus an attic decorated with a series of engaged Composite order columns. Fancy as can be. Through the windows, I could see women in fox and ermine stoles and men in white ties and tails. Not in a million years could I walk through the front door.

A delivery truck was parked across the street. The pavement around it was all wet. Leaning against the cab, smoking and wearing a newsboy cap, was a young man, skinnier and taller than me.

"Hey," I said, "I know you. You're Harry Fong's boy."

He straightened up. "Oh, hello, Mr Too."

"How's your dad?"

"He's doing well. What are you doing here?"

I shook the bike handlebars, gave him a big smile. "Mr Sun asked me to see if you needed help."

"He did?"

"Yeah sure. You know Hobbs wants to buy the Seals. And then he wants the Seals to join the National League. Says if things go well, maybe Mr Sun could supply the beer and hot dogs for the ballpark. So tonight's a big night."

"I didn't know that."

"Why would you? Anyhow, that's why he put you in charge, because of how important it is that everything goes smoothly. Everything is going smooth, right?"

The boy gulped so hard he nearly swallowed his cigarette. He put it out on his shoe heel and stuffed the butt in his pocket.

He dusted the ashes off the front of his shirt. "Yeah, sure, Mr Too. Everything is going peachy."

From the corner, a man in tails waved his hands. He could have been mistaken for a guest if he weren't Black and wearing white gloves. Fong's boy nodded and went to the back of the truck. He pulled aside the canvas flap. Inside were crates of champagne buried in piles of ice. I propped the delivery bike against the curb. "Let me take one."

"You sure?"

"Mr Sun sent me to give you a hand, kid."

We each hauled a crate. He had six bottles of Veuve Clicquot. Mine were Cook's. "What's with the cheap California stuff?"

The boy shrugged. "Boss didn't say."

The footman kept waving at us, impatient. We followed him through the back gate on Octavia and down three steps into the crowded downstairs kitchen. He took all six of the Cook's and three bottles of the real stuff. "Crap," I said. "He's mixing the champagne?"

"Never you mind," said the footman. "Take three up to the servery."

"I've got it. You're doing great." I gave Fong's boy a wink.

The back stairwell was dark, narrow, and tightly twisted upwards. I'm a short guy, and I still felt the urge to stoop, it was so cramped. On the main floor, voices, jazz music, smoke, and the smell of booze and perfume wafted to the end of the hall. A White servant in gloves popped out of the servery. He took the Veuve Clicquot bottles. "Tell downstairs more glasses of the other stuff, quick."

"Sure." I winced. "I'm not feeling well. Is there a WC I can use?"

"There's one below beside the back door."

"That one was busy."

The servant sighed. "At the very top of the stairs. And under no circumstances do you go to any other floor."

I didn't spend much time on the second floor, but I will say the Colonel's bedroom, the study, and Mrs Hobbs's bedroom were as beautiful as any quarters I had seen in German castles during the war.

The third floor smelled of strawberry and roses. At the front was a music room. The middle was a guest room with a big Edwardian four-poster bed. The room closest to me had a panelled arched oak door. It was closed, and when I put my ear against it, I heard the distinct sound of ice falling into a tumbler. I stepped in.

The bed had a pink-and-white quilt. The pillows, also pink, were ruffled. Above the headboard, on a yellow-papered wall, hung a number of abstract prints and drawings. Rattan night tables bracketed the bed. On each sat a potted orchid. A young woman in a green silk brocade evening gown looked out a north-facing window towards the bay. Her side-parted chestnut hair was streaked with blonde.

She eyed me up and down and added another cube of ice to her glass.

"I'm sorry, I thought this was the WC."

"There's one there." See pointed to an ensuite. "But I don't believe that's why you're here. I suppose I should scream."

At times like these, I don't bother thinking too much. What to say just pops out of my mouth. "Those are Henry Moores, aren't they?" I pointed to the prints over her bed.

A quizzical look took over her face. "Yes, they are. Why do you know that?"

"I saw a lot of stuff like it. When I was a kid, I took drawing and painting lessons from an old German guy who was keen on my mom. In France, they figured out I knew something about art and spoke the language. Got assigned to a unit that hunted for treasures, you could say."

"Doesn't that make you interesting. They're studies for reclining figures. My father bought them for me when we were in New York. I thought … they were compelling."

"Well, that makes you interesting too. Because some of them, if you look at the bulging orbs, appendages, and orifices, suggest two figures intertwined and not just one."

A bright, wicked smile came over her face. "I thought it was just me. In which ones do you see it?"

I pointed at a convoluted swirl of pencil and wax crayon lines. "There's more than Baby and Madonna in some of these."

"I agree," she said. "It's all tops to tails, if you know what I mean." Now beside me, I could see her green eyes light up. The small faint freckles that dotted the bridge of her nose crinkled. She leaned into me. Her confidence reminded me of what it was like to be her age. Knowing it all. Feeling bigger, bolder than you deserved. But then, maybe she could do whatever she wanted. Her house, her father, her life said she could. I took a step back and looked around the room again.

She read me quickly and turned to the bar cart, already on another tack. "Do you want a drink?"

"I do. But aren't you a little young for it?"

"Well, I'm eighteen, and I've been drinking forever. No one seems to mind. Will Scotch and ice do?"

"Yes, thanks."

"So, mysterious intruder, why are you here?"

"Do you know Constance Moy?"

"Yes, I do. Piano girl. Very nice gal."

"Well, Constance says you have her earrings."

"What could she possibly mean by that?"

"It seems at the recital you gave, I assume in the music room, you told her not to wear them during your performance. Was it the violin for you?"

"No, I play cello."

"Constance says you told her they were garish and to take them off. She told me she did so in front of a mirror. I'm guessing it was at that vanity. When the recital was over they were missing. Which I would say is quite odd considering they were so garish."

"Well, they were in *that* context." She turned her body and shifted her weight contrapposto like a model. "But I think jade looks wonderful with this dress."

"It does, Miss Hobbs."

"Lillian." She extended her hand.

"Alex. Nice to meet you, Lillian." Someone was coming down the hall. I continued, "She'd like them back. You see, unlike in a family like yours, a little trinket can mean a lot. Those earrings you're wearing meant enough for her to ask me to help get them back."

"Lillian," a woman called down the hall. "This party is for you, dear."

Lillian called out. "Coming, Mother. Just changing my earrings." She turned back to me. "We're having a party because I'm going to the debutante ball at the Palm next week. Imagine, Alex, throwing a party because I'm going to party."

"Congratulations."

"Thank you. It's my introduction to society. Without it, apparently, I'd be a leper, an absolute pariah."

"Well, I'll buy you a present. But only if you're good and hand me what belongs to Constance."

"Really? I wasn't joking before. I could just scream."

"I guess you could, but I thought we were past all that. Something like this happened to my friend Walter. He was caught with a White girl at the wrong place and the wrong time. A mob grabbed him, beat him pretty good, and dumped him on the other side of the Golden Gate Bridge. But I'm pretty sure the girl's reputation lost some shine. I doubt she attended any — what do they call it? Cotillion? In any case, such a horrible fate for both of us wouldn't be terribly nice."

A smirk drew across her face. At the vanity, she put down her empty tumbler, took off the jade earrings, and replaced them with emerald studs. She sighed into the mirror. "Just as well. They were still too gaudy. I guess I have an appreciation for the oriental stuff. I don't suppose you wish to join us?"

"Maybe not. I'm not dressed good enough for your crowd."

"No, you're not at all. So is this what you do, Alex? Break into people's homes and steal things back like Robin Hood?"

"Not really. I guess I have a flexibility that allows me to, I don't know, do what's needed."

"Sounds terribly improvisational. Wouldn't it be better to know what you're doing and why?"

"Maybe not everyone has the road set out for them."

"If I didn't know better, I would think you're trying to hurt my feelings." She tucked a strand of hair behind her ear. "Tell Constance I'm sorry. It was just a little prank. You're welcome to finish your drink."

Without a backward glance, she left the room. I pocketed the earrings, finished my whisky, went down the rear stairs, and left through the downstairs kitchen. I found Harry Fong's boy by the truck. He looked anxious. "Where were you?"

"I got sidetracked. Looks like you have things under control." I picked up the delivery bike and put it in the back. "The lady of the house said I could have this." I waved a bottle of Veuve Clicquot then uncorked it, took a swig, and started to walk. It was a beautiful summer night.

I went east down Washington, towards Chinatown, turned left at Stone Street, and stopped at the second door from the corner. My place was a mile away from Lillian Hobbs, practically on the same street. It took less than twenty-five minutes to walk, yet from there to here remained whole worlds away.

2.

I lived on the second storey of 17 Stone Street, one of the smaller residential hotels. The rooms were eight by ten feet, and each floor had its own shared kitchen and bathroom. It was quiet. Being a Friday night, the old-timers were upstairs on the third, playing mah-jong. I could hear above me the clacking of tiles on the tables.

Someone was in my room. The lights were on and the door was wide open. Maybe Lillian had a change of heart and called the cops. I emptied the bottle with a final gulp and gripped the neck in my right hand. I stepped in.

Two men in grey suits were rifling through my shelves. They spun towards me. Both were tall with tight crew cuts. One was built like he should hang out at Muscle Beach. The other looked like he could play up front on a basketball team. Their fedoras had been tossed onto the covers on my cot.

The big guy eyed the champagne bottle and looked ready to tackle me. The skinny one put a hand on his partner's shoulder and tried to hold him back.

The big guy grabbed my wrist. I bladed my body to the right and hooked the bottle over his wrist. My free hand came over his and trapped it. I pushed down hard, and he went to his knees. I manoeuvred around and locked his arm behind his back. "I'll break it, Mac."

The big guy grunted, "No you won't." Tried to get out of the hold but couldn't.

"Everyone, settle down," said the skinny one. "Take it easy." He glared at his partner. "Now."

The big guy relented and relaxed. I let go. He got back on his feet and fumed, his fists clenched. There wasn't much room, and room was what I needed. Maybe I could club him hard with the bottle and hope the other guy wasn't too fast.

The skinny one said, "Are you Lieutenant Alexander Too?"

"Who's asking?"

The skinny one pulled out an ONI badge, naval intelligence.

"I'm Special Agent Tasker. This is Special Agent Beatty. We're hoping you can help us with a problem."

"I'm sure whatever problem you have, you can solve it yourself. Now, get out, please." I held open the door. "I've had a long day." I waved the empty bottle. "And I need some shut-eye."

Tasker looked like he was trying to sort out what to say next. He hesitated. "Look, Lieutenant Too."

I interjected, "*Mister* Too. I'm not a lieutenant anymore."

"Okay, *Mister Too*. But matters are quite urgent."

"They always are."

"We were instructed to bring you in."

I tightened my grip on the bottle. If Abbott and Costello were thinking they could haul me to Leavenworth or some other hole, they were wrong.

Beatty started to lean forward. Tasker took a step back and lifted his hands up. "Hold it, there, Mr Too. I was briefed on the possibility you may not want to come in. I don't know what all this is about, but I was instructed to tell you, 'Bekker is alive.' Whatever that might mean."

I took a step back like I had been punched in the stomach. "Who told you that?"

"No one. It just came with orders from the N-2, Twelfth Naval District, to find you. I asked my boss. He said it came down the line, and that's it." Tasker looked at my pitiful sagging cot and my one stool. "Is there somewhere we can talk?"

"Sam Wo's is two blocks down."

My head hurt. I wasn't sure if it was from the champagne or the news. I hadn't heard the name Bekker since the end of the war. I had written him off as a ghost or a rumour among the select few who knew about him. Bekker, the shadow among shadows. And somehow, someone knew I would want to know more.

At Sam Wo's, you had to walk through the noisy kitchen with its blazing gas stoves and clanging woks to get to the dining room on the second floor. Upstairs, you couldn't swing a cat without hitting a customer, but we found a table. Beatty couldn't quite fit in the booth. He had to sit in the aisle, which he blocked with his frame. Waiters had to stretch up to lift the dishes over Beatty's head. Every time a bowl of soup went by, Beatty winced. I liked that.

I ordered the two agents coffee and spring rolls. I stuck with tea and asked for *jook* with pork and liver. Chaotically crowded and noisy, there was no chance of anyone eavesdropping, but Tasker waited until we were served. He scanned all the diners one more time and began. "Okay, Lieutenant——"

I interrupted. "Again, 'Mister' will be fine."

"You're still commissioned. Your file says you're on extended furlough."

"Is that what they're calling it?"

"I don't know what you'd expect. You were born in China."

"To American-born parents," I interjected. "I grew up here."

Tasker pressed on. "You were part of the Sino-American Cooperative Organization in '45 and part of the Dixie Mission until '47, where you worked closely with the Communists in Yan'an."

"As an interpreter and advisor."

"Interesting. The parts of the file I was allowed to see said your specialization was in art objects, antiquities, and artefacts of interest. I don't even know what that means. But I do know we're at war with North Korea, Mr Too, and the Communist Chinese are helping them. Your friends at the Dixie Mission recommended America drop the Nationalists and cooperate with Mao. Does it look like we're cooperating?"

"Funny, I don't recall writing any of those reports, yet somehow I'm guilty by association."

"Look, no offense. This is all a side track. I'm here to get you to consider the future. I've seen your file. It was censored a ton, but I know you joined the army at seventeen, received a battlefield commission at nineteen, and your file has a letter from SHAEF signed by Ike himself, pretty much letting you go wherever you wanted in Europe. Take China out of the equation and your record is exemplary, as far as I can see. Heck, I'm not even allowed to know what you were doing back then, but I do know you wanted to help your country. Yeah, you're out now. I'm offering you a way back in."

"Into what? I don't have a country anymore." I gestured at the tight space of Sam Wo's. "This is my country."

Beatty pushed back his chair and stood up. The waiter nearly spilled a whole meal on the floor and called Beatty a '*bun dan lo fan*'.

"Forget it, Tasker. He isn't our guy."

I was tempted to let them go, but I thought about Doc Parr dashing out of Camp Ashcan near Luxembourg in the spring of 1945 with a name on his lips. It was Parr who recognized my abilities beyond my age or colour. It was Parr who introduced me to a side of reality that I never believed existed except in pulp magazines. It was Parr who made me feel I could make a difference. Parr was a good man. But a few days after he left Camp Ashcan, Parr died in a secret Nazi cave in Northern Bavaria, apparently attacked by wolves. "Tell me about Bekker."

Tasker motioned for Beatty to sit down. "All I know is I'm supposed to tell you he's alive and he's here."

"In the States?"

"San Francisco, Mr Too. Bekker is here. But that's all I have," said Tasker.

"So what do you want from me?"

"There's a set of orders in an envelope waiting for you on a transport. It's sitting on the runway on the other side of the Bay Bridge. You say so, I'll give you a ride and you can read them yourself."

3.

We drove to an isolated hangar on the northwest edge of Naval Air Station Alameda. We rolled in and parked beside a Gooney Bird, a C-47 Skytrain. Beatty and Tasker hung by the sedan, started gabbing with the air crew. I climbed into the cabin.

The plane had side benches on the left and right of the cargo space. At the rearmost seat, I found the envelope. I pulled a file stamped 'TOP SECRET: TOP HAT'. I was impressed with myself—I was both an enemy alien and cleared to read.

I craned to look out the cargo window. Tasker and Beatty remained by the car. The top sheet spelled out my orders:

1. You will pose as a US Navy steward (rank Steward 3rd Class) and serve the residents of Hut 17 at Camp Gumdrop.
2. Observe and report the nature and details of their conversations, especially those carried out in German.
3. Only report to Capt. Cyril Stephenson at evening debriefs after your steward duties are completed. Do not seek Capt. Stephenson or reach out to him in any way. The means and methods of your contact and communication will be determined by Stephenson as the situation allows.
4. Under no circumstance are you to reveal your past military service or qualifications, your language abilities, or any other detail that would make the residents of Hut 17 believe you are anything other than a colored servant.
5. Burn these orders upon reading.

That's all. I had never heard of Camp Gumdrop and there was no mention of Bekker. I went to the open front cargo door and signalled Tasker to come over. "There's nothing here about him."

"I don't know anything about it. All I know is if you say 'yes', I'm supposed to kit you up" — he pointed to a set of tables against the wall of the hangar — "and put you on the plane. Then I make a call to the Officers Club. Tell a guy you're ready. But you have to say so."

I shook my head, thought about it, then nodded. Tasker took me to the tables. They were covered in differently sized navy steward uniforms, boots, and winter coats. Independence Day was less than a week away. "Where the hell am I going?"

Tasker replied by holding up an extreme-cold-weather parka. It had fur around the hood. "This will fit you. Swap out of your civvies."

In half an hour, I was fully kitted, dressed in navy blues like Popeye, and had topped the outfit off with a white cap. I had trouble keeping it on my head. After a year of civilian life, my hair was the longest it had been since I joined the Army. I stepped outside the hangar and dug out my Zippo.

Some guys had engraved lighters that said where they'd been — North Africa, Italy, Normandy, maybe all three — what battles they'd fought, how many fighters they'd shot down. That kind of shit. Mine was entirely blank. If I dropped it or lost it, you would never know to whom it belonged. I held my orders, envelope and all, by my fingertips and ignited the papers. They shrank and curled. I held on until I couldn't bear the heat and let go. The ashen remains floated into the dusk sky.

A set of headlights approached, and a sedan pulled alongside Tasker's. Three men stepped out. Two were Navy. The officers unloaded luggage from the trunk and with it they boarded the transport. The third man was tall but not quite Tasker's height. He was leaner and wore a dark suit, though it was too dim to tell what colour. He didn't wear a hat, and his hair on top was long and slicked back, but the sides were shaved down nearly to the skin. His face was long and horsey. His eyes glinted. He lit a cigarette and looked directly at Beatty, Tasker, and me, but he didn't speak. He just watched us without flinching. He drew on his smoke, tapping off the ashes after every puff. When he was done, he flicked the butt out the hangar door. He reached into the trunk and pulled out what I assumed was a long fishing-rod case. He embarked, and the twin engines fired up.

"You'd better go," Tasker said. "That's your guy."

4.

I've tried to reconstruct the flight. From Alameda, the plane must have taken us to Great Falls Air Force Base, Montana, then to Station Edmonton. We refuelled in Fort St. John, British Columbia. The next hop was to Elmendorf Air Force Base, Alaska, where we switched to a bomber. I think it was a P2V Neptune.

The odyssey by air took around thirty-six hours. We flew farther north and west, and by the second night we entered the land of the midnight sun. At two in the morning the sky became no darker than twilight.

I couldn't doze on the flight and found myself watching the man I assumed was Bekker. It was difficult to be discreet. In the Neptune, we were stuffed in a rear cabin with six jump seats. I was on one side and he was on the other. It would have taken nothing for me to unbelt, walk up to him, and introduce myself, but his two escorts didn't welcome any exchange between us. The few chances we had to stretch our legs on the ground, they seemed to shield him from me, sticking so close to the man, in fact, that I couldn't be sure if he was a VIP or a prisoner. Maybe he was both.

I'll admit I caught myself staring. His ears were mildly deformed and came to slight points. His chin was narrow. His hands and neck revealed pale skin lined with bold blue veins. He looked sick. He returned my gaze a few times, and on each occasion he broke into a mocking smile. It unnerved me.

At one point a crew member offered him a cup of coffee. They had to yell over the sound of the engines, and I overheard some of their exchange. The man spoke with a German accent. From that point on, I was sure he was the person Doc Parr had pursued in the last days of the war.

When Tasker first mentioned Bekker, I hoped I would have a chance to interview or interrogate him, find out what happened to Doc. But now, because of his leering expression and my tiredness, sense of dislocation, and instinct that he was responsible for Doc's death, I decided that if I had the opening to kill this man, I would.

On the second morning, we flew in the clear blue above heavy clouds. Time to time, through the breaks, I spotted mountainous, snow-capped islands, one after the other. We had to have been over the Aleutians. Around noon, the Neptune descended through the clouds. We landed on an airstrip on the island of Attu, taxied to a shack that served as the terminal, and disembarked. It was good to stretch my legs. There was drizzle, and the air was chilly. The Attu summer felt like San Francisco winter. To the south, the ocean practically lapped onto the tarmac. To the north rose grass slopes. Further off I could see huge white peaks draped in thick clouds. It was one of the bleakest places I had ever seen.

Gumdrop: A Bekker Story

A man in crumpled tan pants, a cardigan, and a ball cap ran up to the plane. "I'm here to take you to that," he said, and pointed at a Coast Guard tender waiting just off shore. He looked up and down at Bekker, his escorts, and me. "Hey, guys, just to let you know, up here, most of the time, especially on shore, we don't wear uniforms. Or suits."

Bekker's buddies grabbed his bags and followed our guide. Bekker himself cradled his fishing-rod case and fell back, walking in step with me. He leaned as if speaking in confidence. "Good thing. You simply don't look the role, my friend. And never will. I don't believe there are any barbers where we are going."

I must have shown my confusion.

"Your hair," Bekker said. "I do not believe the US Navy permits — how do you say it? — 'pompadours'."

Before I could stop myself, I touched my hair.

"Nothing is what it seems, my friend," he said, and strutted ahead. I pulled my sailor's cap off my head and followed.

USCG *Sweetbrier* sailed southwest. A young steward directed Bekker to the wardroom, which was reserved for officers. Being a steward as well, I had the option of hanging in the crew mess or remaining on deck. Our final destination, the steward informed me, was just over the horizon. It would be only a two-and-half-hour sail. I decided to stay outside; I'd been cooped up in planes long enough and needed the fresh air. And those few words with Bekker had unnerved me in a way I hadn't been since my first time in combat in France. The steward asked if he could join me. I said, "Sure." The company was welcome. We smoked and talked.

While I had been sworn to secrecy, the Coast Guard sailor was a real yakker. "Wait 'til you get a load of Camp Gumdrop. It's a brand-new island. Don't know if you ever heard about that quake up here in '46. It killed a whole bunch of folks with a tsunami. Hawaii, Washington, California. But that ain't the half of it. You see, it also caused an island to rise up straight out of the ocean. Not joking. They keep telling us it's volcanic, but it doesn't look like that. It doesn't look natural at all. More like someone made it, which is why I suppose it's such a big deal. We've been shipping a whole bunch of Kraut VIP there. I'm pretty sure they're all Nazis, but then, I think they're all Nazis. Anyhow, the Navy and the Coast Guard have their hands full trying to keep the Russians from taking a peek at it. Got a whole task force trying to keep a twenty-mile buffer around it. And get this: you're on the only ship that's allowed to sail to it. We bring all the supplies and personnel to Gumdrop. Done about forty trips this year. But I ain't never set foot on it. Seeing as you're by yourself, no minders or nothing"—he checked to see if anyone else was nearby—"maybe you can tell me what's going on."

"I'm sorry," I said. "This is all new to me."

"Oh shoot, man, then wait until late tonight. These last few nights the sky has been glowing."

"Do you mean the Northern Lights?"

"Nah, I've seen tons of that stuff up here. This is Alaska. No, you don't get that right now because it's summer. It's too bright. No, what you get this time of year is the sky goes grey for a couple of hours and it doesn't get dark enough for auroras. Nah. What goes on over Gumdrop is different. The sky gets stormy right over it, localized, then the light show begins. It's like a spot thunderstorm but wilder. Last night's was a doozy. Maybe even tonight. Watching it is like watching the end of the world, make you flip your lid. So be careful. It can be like looking at the sun too long." He squinted then pointed. "Hey, there it is. That's Gumdrop."

On the distant horizon, through the ocean mist, I saw what appeared to be a listing aircraft carrier. Not like an island at all. As we sailed closer, I realized my sense of scale was all wrong. It was ten, no, twenty times larger than any ship I had ever seen, two miles long and half a mile wide of black rock. There was no way it was geological. It wasn't an island. Gumdrop was a massive leaning obelisk.

As the *Sweetbrier* approached a makeshift pier at the wide base, I could make out a village of shacks, huts, and tents assembled nearby. Up the steep slope towards the peak of the obelisk snaked a trail of ropes passing through the eyes of rock anchors. I saw people clinging onto the ropes to scale the incline, which was about as tough as climbing the hilliest streets back home. Along this precarious path were a series of clustered buildings. The lower clusters had more structures, but they became sparser as the trail reached the top.

Screaming drew my attention back down to the pier. Waiting for us to dock were an officer, the Master-at-Arms, four Marines or guards, and three orderlies and a female nurse holding up a stretcher with a bellowing man strapped to it. "I gotta go," the steward said. "Ain't supposed to see this stuff."

He abandoned me on the deck and retreated through the crew mess door. The screamer was young and dark skinned, maybe Mexican. They hauled him up the gangplank, and I could see his eyes rolling wildly, unseeing. His face was screwed up and contorted. He drooled, sputtered, and wailed. "Close the gate. Save our souls. Close the gate." His raw screams sent a chill down my spine. There was no doubt in my mind that living in a place like this for too long could easily drive a person beyond the brink of sanity.

A boatswain directed the stretcher team into the bowels of the ship, but I could still hear the man's ranting. Bekker emerged on deck, and as he passed me to go down the gangplank, he muttered, "I hope you are not his replacement." He shook hands with the officer and headed towards the main group of buildings at Camp Gumdrop.

I was guided by a Marine and the Master-at-Arms. As we climbed—everything was either uphill or downhill here—I had a chance to get a good look at the black rock. I was never a geologist, but I guessed it was some sort of basalt with streaks of obsidian. It wasn't a new formation, but was old and worn with a polished surface. In fact, it was slippery.

The Master-at-Arms, who was a chief petty officer, gave me the rundown. No one was to move about without an escort. Guards were stationed at each set of buildings along the trail. I was to always stay between the ropes, holding on whenever I could, and never leave the rope trails. Most personnel were assigned one building to live in, one building to work in, and one building to eat meals in. Under no circumstances was I to enter any other building without express permission from the camp commander, a project leader, a department leader, or the Master-at-Arms himself.

There were three exceptions. In an emergency, personnel were directed to rally in the town square, and by that he meant the courtyard formed by the collection of buildings at the base of the trail. The other two places I could enter were the infirmary—he pointed at a white Quonset hut with a red cross painted on it—or the guardhouse—he pointed at a green shack with a small flag flying from it. He added, "If you fall in the water, no one is going to get you. You will survive for thirty seconds, and then you will be dead. Understand?"

I answered, "Yes, Master."

At the edge of town, I noticed a paddock of cattle. "Is that for fresh meat?"

The Master-at-Arms made a grim expression. "No." It was better not to press.

He led me into a barracks building called the Gumdrop Hotel and told me it was later than I realized. I would spend the night here. I could grab breakfast in the mess and by 0700 two guards would take me up to Hut 17. He instructed me to dress in fatigues — it would be a long climb. He paused and added, "If you hear trampling outside or see ropes, rope anchors, or any buildings or structures being moved or knocked down, inform the first officer you can find."

"Trampling outside, Master?" I asked.

"That's right, sailor. You'll know it if you hear it."

I had a bunkroom to myself. I didn't bother undressing. I closed the curtains as tightly as I could and dreamt about all the nameless things that could trample unseen in the twilight.

5.

Hut 17 sat near the end of the great leaning obelisk, nearly a thousand yards above the water. If you were brave enough to stand at the edge, you could watch seabirds fly under you. Eventually, I would think, you would lose your mind.

The building itself was a typical War Department barracks. Enormous resources had been expended to build it here, in the middle of the northernmost reach of the Pacific Ocean and half a mile in the sky. It had two floors and a pitched roof. Its homey paned windows looked incongruous against the churning grey mists and the ominous black rock.

All the Nazi bigwigs lived and worked here, and they were pampered: the mess tables had linens; we used a Navy silver service. I worked with five other coloured people. The Chief Steward and the cook, Hank, were Black. There were two housekeepers, both women. Margaret was Black. Lydia was from the Philippines. Auggie, my fellow steward and roommate, was Chinese like me.

We served twenty researchers at the hut. All of them spoke German, even if they were American. They assumed none of the staff could understand what they were saying, but I did.

I picked up quick that most were Nazis brought over in '45 and '46. In fact, some of them had been on target lists for my old unit, Zero-Kilo Squad, which Doc Parr led.

Doctor Parr had been a full-bird colonel but preferred just 'Doc'. He led our small team that was part of the Allied Command's T-Force in Europe. T stood for 'Technical', and T-Force's job was to track down Hitler's wonder weapons — V-2 rockets, biological weapons, super-soldier serums, that kind of stuff — and the people behind them.

Parr's gang, the one I was in, was more specialized. Zero-Kilo Squad was actually a platoon. Our task was to capture the occult artefacts that had been of interest to the Third Reich and would be of interest to the Soviets. Before Parr disappeared, we had secured three different maps purporting to show the exact location of Atlantis, two versions of the Spear of Longinus, a ring that made the wearer beautiful to any beholder, and a massive clay golem Parr nicknamed Frank.

What began to creep up in our operations were references to a man in black, or 'the man in a long black coat'. More than anything, Parr wanted to find this mystery man, who seemed to be connected to every occult operation ever conducted by the SS. He was at the nexus of all the dark arts being practised in Europe during the war.

And now he was here with me at the edge of the world with a bunch of Nazis I had been trained to track, capture, interrogate, and kill. I couldn't believe I was now pouring them cups of coffee and bringing them sandwiches at their desks.

Of all the Nazis there, I despised Heinrich Kriech the most. He was versed in languages and translation, but he also fancied himself a sorcerer. I had read files that had been hidden in Bavarian caves that confirmed Kriech practised blood magic rituals on POWs and ill slave labourers.

The house staff noticed my disdain.

After my third day of clumsily trying to fulfil the role of a steward, I was brought into the fold of the house staff. At the end of the day, around ten at night, they gathered around the crew mess table in the back and went over the day's events. I was invited to join. The Chief had smuggled a few bottles of Canadian whisky into the hut, and we each nursed a thimbleful of the hooch.

Auggie, the steward, pointed at me and smiled. "I saw you do it. Kriech snapped his fingers at lunch, over and over. Everyone could hear. You ignored him. Everybody in the room stared at you, and you did nothing." He turned to the housekeepers, Lydia and Margaret, and explained, "Alexander made a face like nothing was happening. All relaxed and bored, and he takes two steps behind Kriech. He said, 'Yes, Dr Kriech.' Kriech goes,

'Coffee, Alexander.' He reaches for the carafe just inches in front of Kriech. Kriech says, 'No, Alexander.' He's hissing like a snake when he says, 'It is not fresh.' So Alexander takes two steps back, gets a full one from the credenza. He pours him a hot steaming cup until it starts spilling into his saucer." Auggie slapped his knee like it was the greatest thing he ever saw. "Kriech's face goes totally red. Like he's going to blow a gasket, but everyone is watching, so he says, 'Thank you, Alexander'."

Margaret looked concerned. "Be careful with Kriech. He has a real mean temper. He slapped me once because I knocked over some books. And he yelled, 'Due dumb footsies', or some such at me. Don't know what it means, but I know it wasn't nice."

It wasn't.

The Chief said, "What's your story, anyhow? If we were on board, I would have my boot up your ass. You know nothing about mess or steward duties."

I replied, "I got busted out of my trade. I used to be a mechanic."

Hank, the cook, said, "That's the fucking Navy right there. No second chances for the coloured folk. They don't want us doing any other job but the cooking and cleaning."

The Chief proceeded to recount how he once shot down a Zero after taking over a fifty-calibre during the Battle of the Philippine Sea. Everyone else groaned. Apparently, they'd heard it before.

Lydia shifted the discussion. "What I really want to know about is the strange White man."

"What strange White man?" asked Auggie. "They're all strange."

"Put a cork in it. I'm serious. I've seen him around, creeping outside the ropes with a sword."

Margaret said, "Do you mean the other new guy?"

I interrupted, "When did you see him with a sword?"

"Nights. Or what is supposed to be night. I can't sleep with the sun up like this. So sometimes I sit here in the kitchen and look out the window. I've seen him walking outside the ropes, looking or hunting for something."

I said, "Could he be looking for lost cows?"

Everyone's face at the table lost colour.

The Chief said, "Around two weeks ago, the professors started bringing them up here. Two in the morning they were up, and they went to the end, to the point. That's when the light show happened."

Lydia added, "Summer solstice. Longest day. I remember exactly. I couldn't sleep at all that night."

The Chief continued, "The professors came back all bloody. All the cows were gone."

"What did the American professors say?" I asked.

"What do you mean? They were doing it too." He shivered. "Let me pour you all another." This time we all got more than a thimble.

"That's why you're here, Alexander," Auggie said. "The guy before you snuck out to see what was going on. He came back, but he was not all right in the head anymore. Talking about all sorts of nonsense. It got so bad, we sent him to town. You replaced him."

"I heard him screaming about a gate," I said.

"More nonsense than that," Auggie replied. "He talked about floating eyes, and cities underwater, and women having baby monsters."

Margaret said, "It's terrible what happened to him. But the wild look was in his eyes. All the professors in Hut 17 have it."

"All of the professors here have gone to the end of the obelisk?"

"Uh-huh," Margaret confirmed.

"Have any of you?"

All of them shook their heads except Lydia.

"Have you?" I repeated.

"Like I said, I don't sleep so good. Sometimes I sleepwalk. I woke up there three nights ago."

Hank whistled. "You okay?"

"I didn't see anything."

I had to ask. "Did you hear anything?"

Lydia cast her eyes down. "Yes. I heard something behind me. I tried to run back to the hut. Something knocked me down. I woke up back in my bed."

"Do you know who put you there?"

"Maybe the man with the white hair, the man with the sword?" Lydia offered.

Auggie teased, "You're probably pregnant with a monster now."

Hank punched him in the shoulder. "That's not funny."

"You know what's funny?" Auggie retorted. "We're in the middle of the Pacific Ocean, with a bunch of Nazis and crazy *gweilo* Americans, feeding cows to a monster that fell from a hole in the sky."

When the cooking and cleaning staff went to their berths, I stayed behind in the galley. I tried to compose my thoughts. What did I know? What were suppositions? What conclusions could I draw?

From men like Kriech, I only heard the banal details of translating hieroglyphs in the stones, the recording of sudden barometric changes, whether the lights above the tip of the obelisk could be captured on regular or infrared film. What I overheard could almost convince me nothing monstrous was taking place. But our gossiping crew of servants could see the horror of it all.

To whom could I pass on this intelligence? My fourth day at Gumdrop was about to start and I had yet to come across Captain Cyril Stephenson, my contact. Was he already in Hut 17? He could have been one of the American researchers, or even a German one. Maybe he was the Chief but it wasn't the right time to reveal himself? He could be anyone, I supposed. But I couldn't just wait. Whatever research they were conducting here had gone off the rails.

As twilight faded into another long day, I decided to hell with orders. The next grey night, if the coast was clear, I would sneak to the tip of Gumdrop and see what the big deal was all about.

6.

Kriech was in a foul mood the whole day. One of the project leads, a sonic scientist who believed he could probe the depths of the obelisk with sound waves, had gone missing.

The Master-at-Arms, who served as the base's chief of police, and the camp commander, who lived in town, came up to confer with Kriech and the American head of research.

While I brought them pound cake and coffee, I listened to Kriech complain. "You have totally lost security at this camp. People are moving beyond the ropes, letting themselves into our zone of research. Then we have to consider the issue of our missing specimen. Do you realize how precious it is? That *bisher* is the greatest fruit of our labours here these two years. And now you can't return it to us."

The Master said, "How do you expect us to find something that's invisible?"

Kriech slammed the table. "Science. Herr Doktor Schrader has given you optical devices to see beyond normal human wavelengths. Employ them."

"They're clumsy and heavy. Sometimes they don't work."

"That is slander! These inventions if we had them during the Battle of the Ardennes, Germany would have sent the Allies back to the English Channel. You should be grateful you have them instead of the Russians."

The camp commander turned to the American head of research and pleaded, "We're doing everything we can."

The American researcher said, "I'm sorry. I agree with Dr Kriech. You need to fix this."

"Well, the Master here thinks it's attracted to the cattle in the lower pen. He thinks we can trap it down there or bring all the cattle up here to catch it."

Kriech said, "Finally, an idea from you that might actually accomplish something. Unlike your idea to bring in your own consultant."

The Master said, "Who do you mean?"

"Bekker! That is who. I have a spyglass up here. I saw him debark onshore four days ago, and I recognized him instantly. Do you know what he really is? He is an exterminator. He will not capture our specimen. He will kill it."

"That's not true. We gave him specific instructions to capture the specimen."

"Herr Master-at-Arms, he has never cared about orders — even from the *Führer* himself. Why would he care what you say?"

The camp commander promised to send up the cows with a squad of guards. He would also talk to Bekker about the scope of his mission or transfer control of the consultant to Hut 17.

Kriech spoke in German to the American head of research. «When Bekker comes up, we will kill the swinedog.»

The American researcher cleared his throat and said in English, "That would be fine. Please send Bekker up here. I want him under my supervision."

The camp commander said, "Fine. We'll do it that way if it makes everyone happy."

Kriech said, "It does. It will."

7.

That evening, a thick bank of clouds engulfed Gumdrop, blotting out the midnight sun as it skimmed just below the horizon. A heavy rain poured, and the darkness of night descended over the island.

The Hut 17 crew decided they would not conduct any 'experiments' at the tip of the obelisk, which frustrated Kriech. For everyone else, even the mad-eyed 'professors', a tension was released. I felt it. An anxiety had been eating at my guts since I had arrived. But I hadn't noticed it until this night, until it had been lifted. Maybe we were in the eye of the storm.

After the researchers' dinner and all our evening duties were done, the cooking and cleaning crew ate a roast by candlelight. Auggie asked if it was a demon cow. At the Chief's behest, we finished the last of his Canadian whisky. Everyone turned in early, even Lydia.

I was lucky. Auggie snored, and I knew he was out until morning. I dressed and snuck into the kitchen. Hank liked to cook with a big fourteen-inch knife. I took it with me. With the cloud and the downpour, it was as dark as a moonless night. It took a while for my eyes to adjust. I found the rope-lined path, grabbed on with my left hand, and started up the slope to the end of the obelisk.

The smooth obsidian had become even more slippery. I fell and smacked my head on the stone surface. I was lucky I didn't impale myself on Hank's knife. I scrambled to my feet and touched my wet forehead. It wasn't just rain—I was bleeding. As I climbed, a buzzing swelled in my ears and I found it hard to breathe. I was certain something beyond the ropes was watching me. I tried to stop my heart from racing, but couldn't. The only thing I could do was climb. Sliding my feet against the slick rock, pulling myself along the rope with my one hand—I was unwilling to put the knife in my other hand down—I worked my way to the summit.

A static charge filled the air, and all the hairs on my arms stood up. The obelisk peaked into a pyramid shape. I stepped carefully onto one of the triangular faces. It angled down to the unseen ocean below and declined more steeply than the climb upwards. I bent down and groped with my hands. Hieroglyphs seemed to be carved into the rock. Without them, I probably would have slipped and slid right into the ocean. A lightning strike hit the tip of the obelisk, and silhouetted against the brilliant white light was Bekker. He wore a long coat that flapped in the wind. He held his sword in one hand, and in the other, quite unbelievably, a harness attached to a cow.

"Ah, is that you, Mr Pompadour?" he said. "Good evening."

"What are you doing here?"

"What does it look like I am doing here?"

"I don't know."

"I'm here to fish. And I brought bait. And you?"

"I wanted to see."

"And what do you think?"

I said, "It's the most terrible thing I have ever seen … this place."

"I concur."

"I knew Doc Parr."

Another stroke lit the scene. Bekker smiled. "I met him once."

"I know. What happened to Doc?" I asked.

"He helped me stop something terrible." Bekker looked at my knife. "Do you wish to help me stop something terrible?"

"How can I trust you?"

"Nobody ever does. But Doctor Parr did."

"And he died."

"But not in vain." Another bolt slashed down behind him. He asked, "What is your name?"

"Alexander Too. Are you actually Bekker?"

"That is what the Nazis call me."

"You are a Nazi."

"Ha. I am not even Aryan. Why would I wish to be a Nazi? I know there is some pithy adage about the company a person keeps, but perhaps it is not quite correct. If my race matters to you so much, as far as I can recall, I am Rouran. I came from Mongolia a long, long time ago."

"Never heard of them."

"We were conquered by Turkic nomads and absorbed. Which is the way of things. The search for purity is quite exhausting and ridiculous. Consider the situation we find ourselves in now. Do you not think it is contradictory for a so-called master race to spend so much energy seeking powers from the beyond? If they are so perfect, why do they need weapons or magics or relics of any kind? I have never understood it."

"I'm not here to philosophize, Bekker."

"Then what are you here for?"

Like I said before, at times like these, I don't think too much. Maybe I didn't trust Bekker, but I did trust my instincts. "I want to close the gate."

"Good stuff. We will, Mr Pompadour, but first we have to attend to another matter. You see, this cow—which, I should add, was difficult to bring up here—and that terrible gash on your forehead have attracted the spawnling that has been causing a commotion among the folk of this camp."

Something was behind me. I spun around, Hank's knife ready. Rain pelted my face. I heard the wind and waves, smelled the salt of the air and the faint rot from the ocean. I could not see Bekker's prey. But I knew it was there. It had stalked me from the second I'd left the hut, I was sure. Blood pounded in my ears. Bile built in my throat.

"Face me. Come forward carefully," commanded Bekker. "That's it. Do not turn around. Keep your eyes on me."

Space and geometry seemed to bend at the tip of this ancient monolith. I'd climbed to reach the pyramid atop the obelisk but now had to climb down to reach the Man in the Long Black Coat. I groped with my heel and toe to find solid footing in the grooves of the carved glyphs. Light flashed across the sky. The ancient words and symbols hewn into the glassy stone held a glow.

"That is very good, Mr Pompadour. Keep your eyes on me."

Bekker's own eyes looked over my shoulder, beyond me. They widened. Was it surprise, wonder, or derision that etched on his face? I'm still not sure if he was addressing the unseen now made visible behind me, or the sickly green radiance that had begun to swell around us.

"Yog-Sothoth knows the gate. Yog-Sothoth is the gate. Yog-Sothoth is the key and guardian of the gate. Past, present, future, all are one in Yog-Sothoth. He knows where the Old Ones broke through of old, and where They shall break through again. He knows where They have trod earth's fields, and where They still tread them. He knows why no one can behold Them as They tread."

The cow pulled the harness, and Bekker lost his grip. The poor beast's eyes bulged. It bellowed, afraid, as if it knew it was going to be slaughtered. Its hooves began to slip, and the animal tilted down to the deadly edge. It went over. Something knocked me from behind, and I fell to the ground. Hank's knife clattered and slid down into the black.

Bekker stood over me. He raised his blade above his head and cackled. I thought he had lost his mind, that he would swing his weapon down and end my misery. I closed my eyes tight.

He cried out, "*Tirra-ma a-lu-ti' i a kaiiapti Saru-hi-a i-pu-Su iu-pi-i, ar-kii up-pn-US kikittzi Suriti lu ina I lz zna sZri ellziti tanaddi kakkara tax-abbi …*"

In my mind flashed images of orbs floating among stars and peering through a rip in the sky where the sun dawned and clouds melted away. I opened my eyes to see Bekker looking down at me.

"Mr Pompadour, are you all right?"

I stood up. "I think so."

The whole of Gumdrop shook. I nearly lost my balance. "It is beginning to sink," Bekker said. "But do not worry. It will most likely take a number of days."

He put an arm around my torso to support me, and we made our way off the pyramid. We crested and began to descend the long downward slope towards Hut 17. All the residents of the barracks had started to file up the rope path.

Kriech led the way, dressed in his bathrobe, with a dozen other Nazis behind him. He screeched, "What have you done?"

Bekker replied, "I brought you a cow, but it fell."

Kriech pushed past us and made for the end of the obelisk. The researchers, Nazi and American, followed. The Chief and the rest of the cooking and cleaning crew stood, stunned.

"Have you all eaten?" Bekker asked. "I think I will make eggs."

He sat the Chief, Hank, Auggie, Lydia, Margaret, and myself down at the table, poured us coffee, and served us toast and eggs.

The crew peppered him with questions about the lights, the invisible stalker, the seismic shift that had just occurred. He avoided answering. Instead he directed their attention to me. "Did you know Mr Pompadour here is a spy?"

"On us?" the Chief said.

"Oh dear, no. On the residents of this charming place."

They asked if I spoke German. I told them yes. Margaret asked what 'due dumb footsies' meant. I translated. She retorted, "Well, Kriech is a mealy-mouthed son of a gun who still stains his sheets."

Bekker was about to pour us another round of joe when a bespectacled guard stepped into the crew mess.

"Good morning, Stephenson," Bekker greeted.

I looked up at my disguised contact. He nodded back at me. Bekker asked, "Would you like some eggs?"

Captain Stephenson was about to reply when we heard a loud crack, and the whole island shuddered. We all clambered out of the barracks.

Gumdrop's entire hieroglyph-covered summit had cracked off and plunged the half mile into the ocean, taking Kriech and the researchers of Hut 17 with it. Bekker recommended we climb down to the base of the island. No one argued.

In a few hours, the whole of Camp Gumdrop was under evacuation. The *Sweetbrier* and two ships from the screening task force ferried hundreds of personnel to Attu before the end of the day.

A small team stayed ashore to destroy any records and equipment that couldn't come aboard, but they were lucky to get off Gumdrop in time. Great portions of the obelisk continued to shear off into the water.

It took two and a half days to sail to Anchorage. Before we docked, rumour was Gumdrop had crumbled to the bottom of the ocean without a trace.

8.

When I returned home to San Francisco, I had some loose ends to tie up. First I visited Constance and returned her jade earrings. She told me they had belonged to her grandmother and had always brought the family good luck. I told her I hoped they would continue to do so.

Then I had a Chinatown jeweller do me a custom job, which I wanted to drop off at the Hobbses'.

If it hadn't been for my uniform and bars, I don't think the valet would have let me in. I waited on the settee in the foyer.

She came down the stairs. "I had to see what he could possibly mean by 'a caller by the name of Captain Too', and I can hardly believe it. Is that Mr Robin Hood?"

"One and the same, Lillian." I held out a small box.

"For me?"

I nodded. "Obsidian. I hope it's elegant enough for you."

"Yes, it is. I like the mounting. But it doesn't go with my eyes."

"No, but it perfectly matches your heart."

"Still trying to hurt my feelings, I see."

"I doubt that's possible. Actually, I thought you should have it because I'll never be able to look at a Henry Moore without thinking of you."

"That's sweet. I don't think you've crossed my mind once."

"I didn't expect so, hence the memento."

"Well, thank you. The sheen on it is out of this world."

"You don't know the half of it."

"Would you like a drink?"

"It's best I be on my way. I have a car waiting out front."

Lillian held open the front door. "Is there a war you're late for?"

"You could say. Have a nice life, Lillian. Try to be good."

"I will, Captain Too."

I did my damnedest not to turn around before I heard the door shut.

Bekker sat on the passenger side of the black Bel Air Sport Coupe. "Nice house. Who lives there?"

I loosened my tie and tossed my garrison cap to the back. "I'm not sure."

§

The invocation to Yog-Sogoth is from 'The Dunwich Horror' by HP Lovecraft, first published in Weird Tales, April 1929.

FEATURE INTERVIEW

JJ Lee

Pulp Literature: *You begin 'Gumdrop: A Bekker Story' by situating us in the historically distant but still recognizable world of early 1950s San Francisco. You then lead us deftly and seamlessly to a world of espionage and intrigue, and finally to a world saturated with delicious (though perhaps not appetizing!) horror-fantasy elements. How do you get so many worlds into so few words?*

JJ Lee: Necessity. I wanted a character and a setting that could address the white supremacy explicit in Lovecraft and in the kind of fantasy and adventure I've always loved in print stories, comics, and film. To me, we have a noir-light hero, in Alexander Too, experiencing anti-Asian racism, early McCarthyism, and the same dislocation a lot of Asians in North America do. Alex is the character by which I hope to de-program myself. It's a process and not perfect, but I'm on it.

PL: *As an Asian-American veteran and spy in mid-twentieth-century San Francisco, Alex Too inhabits a multitude of cultural spaces. Could you tell us about the inspiration for this instalment of The Man in the Long Black Coat, and about how Alex came to be?*

JJ: Several sources. Awkwafina is one. Her articulation of what it means to be Asian American in her series *Awkwafina Is Nora*

From Queens meant a lot to me. And I wanted my own character to do the work. I also feel Alex comes from William Powell's portrayal of Nick Charles in the *Thin Man* movies. Finally, Alex is Elvis / James Dean by way of my father. My father wore a James Dean–style Baracuta coat and a pompadour in his youth, and I wanted to evoke the brashness my dad exhibited when he was young. Recently, my great-aunt told me he was a total party animal and got himself into lots of situations with his mouth.

PL: *'Gumdrop'——an awesome code name. How did you come up with it?*

JJ: Pure secrecy discipline. In the movies, code names often reflect the secrets they keep. But the proper way to give a code name is to make it completely unrelated to the secret. So it was absolutely arbitrary.

PL: *We first met the Man in the Long Black Coat (aka Bekker) in Issue 8, and then again in Issue 24. We are delighted that you have another military-mystery-monster mash-up for us, and that this seems to be becoming a franchise. Where do you want to send Bekker next? Can we look forward to a collection of stories?*

JJ: LA, baby. Alex and Bekker are hooking up with a more mature John Heck to tackle a JPL rocket scientist mixed up with Satan.

PL: *I came upon a quote of Rumi's, "Language is a tailor's shop where nothing fits," and knew I had to ask you, as both a writer and sartorialist, to offer your reflections.*

JJ: I'll say this—a writer has something in mind. They write words to manifest what's in the mind, but words are their own thing. They have their own reality and there's no way to make the thing-thought appear on the page exactly the way the writer wants. What is imagined will be different from what is manifested.

PL: *As both a writer and an instructor with the Writer's Studio at SFU, how does writing and the teaching of writing intersect for you?*

JJ: I try to back up my teaching with doing. I fully employ techniques that I urge students to use. It's always easier to give writing advice than to write itself, and I find by adopting my own advice I'm saving myself a lot of hassle. To be honest, I don't have a lot of ego about my style, or whatever you want to call it. I just want how it reads to work.

PL: *Is there any of your own advice that you don't follow? Any of your own rules that you break?*

JJ: I'm not much of a plotter or schematics kind of person. I teach students about beats. Sometimes I wonder if I hit them all myself.

PL: *How do you approach research for your work, whether it be for a short story, an essay, or an art piece? How does research for fiction differ from what is required when memory mining (or memory confirming) for memoir?*

JJ: Research is big for me. Especially for the Man in The Long Black Coat stories. I need to get the moon phases right. I need sunset and sunrise to be correct. Even the seating arrangements on the airplanes in the story have to be spot on. Plus, I'm pretty sure you can Google Map exactly where Alexander Too lives. I can't write without historical and geographical details being correct. I would have nearly nothing to say without research. Same goes for memoir. I use facts to springboard myself into memory. Any concrete detail in memoir can become a wellspring of detail for the rest of the memory. A remembered or researched fact can function as a pinpoint light on the stage set of a memory. From there, the memoirist only needs to move the light around to see the rest of the memory.

PL: *As a writer of memoir, short stories, and essays, and as a visual artist, how, for you, do these creative pursuits inform one another? Are there any other artistic forms or genres you would like to explore?*

JJ: I'm still trying to write a proper crime novel. If I could do it right, I'd be a happy human.

PL: *And now, the obvious question: what are your favourite memoirs?*

JJ: The collection by Michael Chabon, *Manhood for Amateurs*. I can't escape its influence on me.

PL: *As we emerge from life in a pandemic, what words of advice might the 2022 JJ have for the 2019 JJ?*

JJ: STOP PLAYING *WORLD OF TANKS*.

PL: *Thank you for taking the time to speak with us. Before we go, one last question: what are you working on now?*

JJ: I want to write about the dishware in my house. Seriously. It's about mixing and matching, cracks and chips, and the kind of shabby life I've lived. Quite sad, really.

SELECTED BIBLIOGRAPHY

'For Memoirists', in *Resonance: Essays on the Craft and Life of Writing*, eds. Andrew Chesham, Laura Farina, Anvil Press, 2022.

'The Man in the Long Black Coat: Bekker', *Pulp Literature* Issue 24, Autumn 2019.

'Nine Acres', in *The Group of Seven Reimagined: Contemporary Stories Inspired by Historic Canadian Paintings*, ed. Karen Schauber, Heritage House, 2019.

'Desdemone', *Pulp Literature* Issue 17, Winter 2018.

'The Boy Who Climbed Trees', in *The Summer Book*, ed. Mona Fertig, Mother Tongue, 2017.

'The Man in the Long Black Coat', *Pulp Literature* Issue 8, Autumn 2015.

'Built to Love,' *Pulp Literature* Issue 2, Spring 2014.

The Measure of a Man: The Story of a Father, a Son, and a Suit, McClelland and Stewart, 2011.

PRETTY LIES: FLY AWAY

Mel Anastasiou

Mel Anastasiou *is a novel acquisitions and story editor with* Pulp Literature Press, *and she co-founded* Pulp Literature *magazine in 2013. Mel helps writers develop through her structural editing, the popular 'Writing Muse' Twitter feed, and two workbooks,* The Writer's Boon Companion: Thirty Days Towards an Extraordinary Volume *and* The Writer's Friend and Confidante: Thirty Days of Narrative Achievement. *Her fiction includes the Hertfordshire Pub Mysteries, the Monument Studio Mysteries, and the Stella Ryman Mysteries, for which she won a Literary Titan Gold book award and was longlisted for the Leacock Medal.*

Fly Away

Part 3. It's the golden summer of 1974 in Howe Sound, BC. Inspired by the story of Orpheus and Eurydice, Jenny Riley searches for entry to the ghost world to find her dead love, Joey, and bring him back. These attempts have put her in mortal danger, and are more hindered than helped by the ghost of a young woman with her own agenda.

Chapter 8

Bowen Island, BC
July 1974

Frances set up her deck chairs side by side. She gave Jenny a cup of coffee and lectured her, at length and at volume, on boat safety. Jenny took the opportunity to do some logical thinking about seeing ghosts.

She set her coffee on Frances's deck rail, leaned forward in her chair, and rested her chin on her fists. The sky over Corner Bay gleamed delft blue. The nine o'clock ferry to Langdale chugged by, white against Gambier's coniferous coast.

Frances elaborated on her theme. "You don't just stand up in a rowboat. One hand for the ship, one hand for yourself. How could you be so careless?"

"I have no idea." Jenny was hard-pressed to keep a neutral expression on her face, because a balloon of excitement was expanding in her head. The impossible had flown from the realm of her imagination and landed squarely in reality because she hadn't imagined nearly being drowned. She had truly nearly drowned. And the blame lay with Moira, the young woman who walked across the water.

Moira, the ghost. Who rose up dry out of the water, and whose weight had rocked the rowboat. Whose foot had even bumped hers—a small thing, so small that Jenny couldn't overlook it. The solid pressure of that strappy shoe against her runner was a sort of physical memory, like the pain of a fall or the heat of a kiss.

Set aside the fact that most people thought that believing in ghosts was for nutjobs. Instead, remember that a minority believed, and had always believed, in ghosts and a ghost world. Take for example the story of Orpheus pursuing his Eurydice into Hades to get her back. That enduring tale showed that the ancient Greeks believed in ghosts. And the ancient Greeks were not fools. They were bright, and right, about mathematics and logical thought. What if they were right about a ghost world, too?

If the ancients were right, then Moira had come from the ghost world. Come from it, and returned to it. What else, and who else, might be found there?

Together forever.

Frances was saying, "And you may not drive my Galaxie, either. It's a ton of deadly metal."

"I have a question," Jenny said.

"About safety? About staying alive while you're visiting me?"

"About the beliefs of the ancient Greeks and Romans."

"For heaven's sake, have you heard a word I've said?"

"Every word you've spoken is indexed in my brain for quick reference. But I want to leave the subject of boat safety for a moment. You know everything about ancient Greece."

"There's an eight-hundred-year span of that history, pre-Homer, about which nobody knows a damn thing. But go ahead."

"Exactly how did Orpheus get into the ghost world to try to bring Eurydice back? Does anybody know?"

"Everybody knows. He crossed the River Styx."

"On foot?"

"On death's ferryboat. And he took a coin to pay the ferryman."

"Like BC Ferries, then."

"What a comic parallel," Frances said coldly.

"But what if Orpheus could have walked over the water into the ghost world?"

"Walk across the River Styx? He couldn't. Anyway, he didn't." Frances blinked.

"That we know of." Jenny rose from the deck chair, set her coffee cup down on the porch rail, and stepped off the deck onto the mossy rocks between the house and the bay. "I've got to go and try something. Thank you for caring about my safety."

"I'm not finished caring," Frances said. "I have lots more caring things to say. Like, can I trust you with kitchen knives?"

Jenny selected a spot on the beach out of sight of Frances's deck. She stood poised on a rock at the water's edge. A light wind brushed her hair back. The tide was in, and water covered most of the barnacles and jagged rocks in the bay. Above her the sun brightened alder leaves, which in turn reflected green and white back onto the water. Despite the breeze, the surface of the water rippled only slightly.

One could imagine walking across water as flat as this.

Jenny stepped into the shallows. She wished she hadn't lost her sneakers, but flip-flops would serve. She wore shorts and a T-shirt, and if this experiment worked, she would stay dry. A sensation of freedom cooled her from head to toe. She hadn't eaten breakfast, and she felt light, as if built from plywood or balsa.

She lifted her left foot and set it down on the surface of the water. Stork-like, she took her weight on her right foot. She raised her arms so slowly that it felt as if they lifted themselves, not through the contraction of the muscles of the arm or back, but by her will alone.

That was surely how a person would walk across the surface of water. By will alone. And once she'd achieved the trick of it, how long before she entered the ghost world?

Jenny curled her toes down, the way a water skier keeps her balance, and teetered there with her foot flat on the surface. The trick was to resist intellectualizing — to suspend her disbelief and convince herself she was up on the surface, running with her feet flat on the top of the water, running so quickly that she had no chance to sink, straight across the top of the water into the green centre of the bay.

She ran forward. Her feet touched bottom, she lost her balance, and she tumbled into shallow waters onto barnacles and small rocks. She sat up, hip-deep in the water, and felt heavy and stupid. It was fortunate that nobody had been watching.

But there on the spit at the end of Corner Bay, lounging under a tree like a skinny Buddha in a yellow T-shirt, sat the young camper named Ketchup. One of Malcolm's, she thought. Well, it wasn't the kid's fault she had failed to walk on water where Moira succeeded. Jenny decided to make the best of being soaked all over. She stood up and waded deeper into the bay.

She called, "Hey, Ketchup, come on in for a swim."

He gave her a look that said, *I may be young but you are crazy*, exhaled with a horse-like noise, and pulled his yellow T-shirt away from his stomach. "Yeah, I don't think so."

She slogged out of the deep and stood shivering, ankle-deep in the water. "Okay. Then I'm going to make a fire. Want to look for firewood with me?"

"That sounds like so much fun." Ketchup closed his eyes. Jenny ran up to the house. Frances was apparently off somewhere in the Galaxie, so without safety lectures to slow her down, she changed swiftly into dry shorts and T-shirt and tucked her folding knife into her pocket. She snatched up a handful of cedar kindling and a box of matches from Frances's hearth.

Back at the bay, she found Ketchup on the beach, tossing rocks into the water. "I'm still not helping."

"Tell you what. I'll ask you a question, and if you answer, you don't have to help."

"Your funeral."

"Do you believe in ghosts?"

"Huh. I hate ghosts."

"Because they're scary?"

Ketchup rolled his eyes. "No. Because ghosts try to boss you and make you do stuff you don't want to do. Like *act terrified*. And *run away*. Not cool."

"Interesting," Jenny said.

"Now you have to answer a question, or else be stupid."

"All right." She braced herself for the question: *What makes you think you can walk across water?*

Ketchup asked, "What is the difference between a duck?'"

"Say again?"

"Don't you know *what* the difference is between a duck?"

"I don't even understand the question."

"Why not?" He was clearly enjoying the exchange.

She forced herself to acknowledge Ketchup's youth and total absence of charm. "Maybe I used to know, but now I'm grown-up."

"Well, poor old you. Then do you want to know the answer?"

"No."

"What is the difference between a duck? One of its legs is both the same."

"Groovy, kid." She chose a spot for the fire just about where her father and Frances always used to build it when Jenny and Rachel were younger, away from the trees so sparks could fly up and pop in the July sky.

She slipped her Swiss Army knife out of her pocket and opened it. She touched the tip of the blade to the cushion of her index finger, where a thin white scar showed against the pink of her skin. *Let's cut our fingers and seal it in blood. Together forever.* It was a good sharp knife still, with two blades and scissors and a useful little removable pick that Joey had lost the first day he'd given it to her. That would have been her twelfth birthday.

Ferry waves startled her back into the present, pounding the coast of Corner Bay so that the spray leapt high against the rocks and splashed down again. She sat on a rock and used the small blade to cut a pile of curly shavings from the piece of cedar kindling. She pulled off several sticks the size of broom straws and laid them lattice-wise across the shavings on the rocky beach. A shadow fell across the shavings, and Ketchup hunkered down at her side.

"The trick," she told him, "is to leave plenty of air space for the fire to feed on."

Children, who knew everything, were hard to impress, but knives and matches apparently made exceptions. Ketchup leaned closer.

"I've got three knives at home better than that," he said.

She cut a pencil-sized stick from the bit of kindling wood and laid it on the shavings. "This is the good part."

She took a match from the box, struck it, and touched it to the shavings. A small flame crept in among the shavings so that they glowed orange and curly like tiny illegible neon signs. The fire gave its first small crackle.

"It's gonna die," Ketchup said.

"Maybe. No, don't touch it yet."

"Fires always die."

Ketchup picked up a twig and pushed at the little pile of shavings, and just as Jenny was certain he'd killed the fire, it caught the broom straws and then the pencil-sized piece on the top.

Ketchup sat back and held out his hand. "Give me the knife. You better let me cut the next size up. Girls shouldn't have knives like that."

"Girls know better than to fall for that argument."

Ketchup, fierce and focused, added larger bits of wood; the flames rose, almost clear against the sunlight. Their moment of shared human triumph over the elements was broken by the sound of quiet cursing among the trees above the beach.

Malcolm thrashed his way through the whippy brush and boughs onto the shore. He carried a large backpack, and he had the air of an explorer who had lost not only his way, but all of his company.

Jenny said, "I think I have one of what you're looking for. Ketchup, here's Malcolm. If you're done with my knife, hand it back."

Jenny held out her hand, and the little boy passed her the knife — handle first, which rather impressed her.

Malcolm asked, "You gave the kid a knife? Do you think that's safe?"

"He did it right. Anyway, your theme is you can't keep people safe."

"No, my theme is you have to try to keep people safe. This whole forest is a death trap. There's no visibility and a million deer trails. It would be so much easier to work at clarinet camp."

"Except for the extraneous tooting," Jenny replied.

"The rule in our cabin, especially after bean supper," Ketchup said, "is *one toot and yer oot.*"

Jenny laughed out loud, and, as if at a signal, Malcolm's yellow-T-shirt campers materialized singly and in small groups from behind and between trees and bushes, drifting across the rocky shore. Cedar branches rattled, and Adrian climbed down a small rock face onto the beach. He sauntered up to Malcolm and Jenny, ran his index finger along Malcolm's left shoulder, across the top of his head, across Jenny's head and down her right shoulder.

"Don't be creepy," Jenny said.

"*C'est plus fort que moi,*" Adrian replied.

"We've got sandwiches in this pack, and there are enough for Jenny, too," Malcolm said. "I've counted the kids twice. All present. Time to hike."

He led the way from Corner Bay up the trail for Mount Gardner. Jenny caught up with him, and the little boys overtook them both and sped up the path and out of sight around a large mossy rock.

Adrian shoved in between Malcolm and Jenny. "This trail goes up. I hate up."

Jenny said, "Save your hatred energy. Islands do rise up out of the sea."

"I also hate smart girls."

Jenny laughed.

"You can't start from sea level and go down," Malcolm told him. "Not without drowning."

Jenny said, "What about Holland? It starts at sea level and goes down."

"Yes, what about Holland?" Adrian asked Malcolm.

Malcolm resettled the straps of his backpack. "Listen, shouldn't we be singing something on a hike? Some kind of camp song."

"Pink Floyd," Adrian suggested. "'Careful with That Axe, Eugene'."

Malcolm said, "Kids can't sing that!"

"It's got no lyrics," Jenny pointed out.

"Now you're catching on."

They rounded a corner and found the kids climbing up and jumping off rotting tree stumps on either side of the trail. Malcolm said, "Stay on the path, kids. There are wasp nests in the fallen trees."

"Cool." Ketchup tore off along the path into the woods. He picked up a branch and smacked at a log. "Wake up, you wasps. Let's see some stinging."

The trail split, and the little boys dashed up the left fork as if by instinct, like salmon or geese. Above their heads the trees closed in, alder and cedar fragrant in the warm mid-morning.

Adrian's steps slowed. "Tell you what I'll do right now."

Malcolm said, "Don't you dare."

"What?" Jenny asked. "Don't you dare what?"

Adrian said, "Nothing. I'm going to go and hug a tree."

Jenny nodded towards the side of the trail. "How about this one?"

The old man's beard cloaking the trunk shone bright green in the sunlight. Adrian stopped and ran a palm down its trunk.

Malcolm said, "You don't care a damn about trees."

Adrian looked off into the forest. "You are wrong. I like to hug trees when I'm alone. I like to find a tree in the middle of nowhere and admire how the light casts green beams along the boughs ..."

"No, you don't." Malcolm caught hold of Adrian's arm. Adrian disengaged himself.

"I said I'd like to be alone." Adrian turned on the heel of his sandal and walked a few paces away and then stopped. He added, "Unless you want to come, smart girl?" He didn't wait for an answer but ambled off, picking up speed as he disappeared among the trees.

"Does he do that a lot?" Jenny asked. "I bet he's always disappearing, isn't he? I have ... I had a friend who acted like that."

Malcolm scowled. "How's your arm? Let me see how that cut is healing."

Jenny held out her arm.

Malcolm looked at it closely and then up at her. "You cut it yesterday. But there's no sign of it."

"Sorry, wrong arm." Jenny pulled away from him and crossed both arms behind her. "Anyway, I was saying that you don't let a friend destroy himself. Adrian, I mean."

"Think I haven't tried? Go ahead, if you think you can do

better. I'm going to see that those kids are all right."

Jenny turned away from Malcolm and followed Adrian into the woods.

Malcolm glanced back at Jenny as she walked off along the path towards the spot where Adrian had disappeared. The slender line of her waist and the curve of the back pockets of her cut-off jeans made him feel unexpectedly happy. He decided he could live with that feeling, because beauty asked nothing of you in return for the pleasure of looking, much the way seeing baby animals raised your spirits, or hearing a good love song cheered up a man who was never going to be anybody's hero.

He turned back to the trail in pursuit of his campers, thumbs looped through the straps of his backpack full of sandwiches. His legs were longer than theirs, but somehow the kids were outpacing him. He sped up.

The plain fact was that Jenny was alone in the woods with Adrian. Malcolm was by nature alert for patterns, so he ought to know that was the way life unfolded. Still, tomorrow would be another day. Anything could happen, and something might.

Back off.

He'd heard these words before, back at camp. Malcolm scanned the woods for a kid hiding behind a tall stump, poised to jump out at him.

Step away and back off.

Malcolm stopped in the middle of the trail. "Shut up."

"You can't make us. Where's the food?" Flash, tiny in his oversized yellow T-shirt, headed the line of boys running back his way.

They swarmed him like ants. Ketchup got behind him and

yanked at his backpack. Malcolm heard the zipper go and swung around.

Ketchup hung onto Malcolm's pack. "Our parents paid you money, so you have to feed us."

"You had breakfast an hour ago," he said.

"We don't care," Tanaka said.

Malcolm wrenched the pack out of Ketchup's hands. "Line up."

Flash said, "We're actually dying of starvation."

"Line up, I said. And sing something."

Two-can growled, "We hate singing."

"Sing something or starve to death." He sounded like Adrian, for which he silently kicked himself. But it worked. Grumbling, they shoved into something like a line. Malcolm dug in the pack for the sandwiches. God knew what would happen when midday rolled around and there was no food left, but surrounded as he was, he had no time for post-apocalyptic thoughts.

"*Honey, you can't love one.*" Tanaka had a bass voice for such a young kid. "*You can't love one and still have fun . . .*"

Malcolm passed out the sandwiches, and the kids tore off the waxed paper and flung it on the ground. They ran off, singing with mouths full. "*Honey, you can't love two. You can't love two and still be true . . .*"

He ripped a bite out of his own sandwich. It was tuna with mayo, so he'd been right to get the sandwiches inside the kids before the day grew too warm and the tuna salad spoiled, and they all spent the afternoon puking into the ferns. But there would be no drama today, no vomiting, and no danger, and all because of a correct decision by Malcolm Lee. He supposed that the world kept on turning because of people like him, who ensured that children were safe and fed. Because of people like him, another generation would grow up healthy and vigorous enough to run out on their responsibilities if they wanted to. He snatched up the waxed paper the kids had dropped on the path and swore to himself.

It occurred to him that Adrian and Jenny had been gone a long time now.

Back off, Malcolm.

"Shut up," he told the voice. He shook his head and made himself hum Andy Kim as he followed the kids up the trail. *"Ain't it good, ain't it right …"*

Back the hell off.

CHAPTER 9

Jenny steadied herself with a hand against the stringy bark of a cedar trunk. In the middle distance, Adrian's yellow head shone among the shadows under the alders and hemlocks. How like Joey he was, this Adrian, with his lazy walk and lost, ironic eyes. The lost ones were always so attractive as they turned and walked away, weren't they? You almost had to follow. You got lost too, but even so, you were sure you could help.

Jenny stepped off the trail and jogged after Adrian. She leapt a rotted red log and brushed through salal bushes that snatched at her bare legs. She followed him between two stands of salmonberry bushes, where small thorns caught at her T-shirt. If she caught up to him, she knew she could make him turn around.

But he was moving ahead so swiftly now that she could hardly make him out among the trees. She tripped over a foot-tall clump of leathery salal, hauled herself up, and ran on. The forest grew thicker with the trunks of cedars and hemlocks. She wished these unreliable deer trails were less bumpy and log-strewn, and she moved with care not to stumble among the conifers and nurse stumps. She lost sight of Adrian completely and slowed to a walk. Ahead she made out a deeper shadow, a gap among the trees, and just beside the gap, a figure she knew well by now. Not Adrian, but Moira.

Perched upon a tree stump, Moira swung her legs, bumping the heels of her strappy shoes against the rotting wood. Behind her, three great cedars leaned together to form a gap in the bush.

"You took your time." Moira stood and brushed at the seat of her summer dress.

Jenny kept several yards of trail between them. "What are you doing here, Moira?"

"Don't be dumber than you need to be. I promised you a party, and here I am. Couldn't you have dolled up at least?" Moira's eye travelled from Jenny's T-shirt and cut-offs to rest upon Jenny's bare toes in her flip-flops. "Listen, sister, there's such a thing as nail varnish."

"And red lipstick?" Jenny asked dryly.

"Deep coral. Do you want to see your fellow or not?"

"My fellow …" Jenny took a step closer. She thought of Orpheus and his Eurydice. "Can you take me to Joey?"

"At least wet your palms and smooth down your hair. Sometimes you don't see past your unpowdered nose, and that's where I come in with advice on men. If you're not sure of your fellow, go to a party where you know he'll be. Flirt, laugh, and look lovely."

Jenny ran her fingers through her hair.

"Is that the best you can do? Well, I guess there's a lid for every pot. Let's hope your fellow is among those present. Welcome to the party."

Moira stepped into the darkness among the cedars. The branches waved once and then hung still. All around Jenny, the forest waited, brown and quiet.

Let's hope your fellow is among those present.

Orpheus had his harp for entry into the ghost world. It seemed that if Jenny had a passport, it was Moira.

Welcome to the party.

Two swift steps took Jenny forward through the gap.

CHAPTER 10

Jenny was only two steps behind Moira when she passed through the dark hole in the forest, but when she emerged, Moira had vanished and Jenny was alone.

She'd left Bowen's forest before noon, but now, on either side of this street, windows shone against night-shadowed yards. Lost blue light from television screens indicated that folk here were settled into prime time. Above the houses to her left, close-packed trees shouldered along steep slopes, and a glimpse of snow among them told Jenny she'd left summer for a colder time of year. She knew this North Vancouver street well, and the Special on the corner lot ahead of her even better. She wished she'd never seen it. She wrapped her arms around herself and wanted warmer clothing.

There was no way she'd go anywhere near Lerner's party house. Jenny turned around with the intention of finding a way back into the midday forest from which she'd come. But the sight of a low-slung car on the gravel verge made her stop. Here stood Joey's father's 240Z. Months ago the Zed, a twisted wreck, had been towed away from the crash site several miles from this place. Now, she took in the sweet, unbroken lines of the car, whole again.

"Joey?"

Jenny yanked open the passenger door. The keys hung from the ignition switch, and the Zed's interior showed no sign of the accident that had killed Joey. The car was empty except for a faded Mexican blanket on the back bench and Joey's empty pre-party mickey of rum on the passenger-side floor. Joey had lasted one week in Boy Scouts back when he was ten, but he'd declared that it taught him that when you came to a party, you came prepared. Moira, Jenny reflected, would say much the same.

Jenny took the car keys and tucked them into her shorts pocket. She shut the Zed's door and turned towards the stucco North Vancouver Special across the street. There was no avoiding it now, as there had been no avoiding it when Joey was alive. Her flip-flops slapped against the blacktop as she walked towards Lerner's house. At least, she always thought of this house as Lerner's. But Lerner was only taking care of it for his aunt, curating the party house that Joey and other friends frequented. Lerner's aunt had put the place up for sale after the accident, not because of Joey's death after the party, but because she saw the mess Lerner had made of it. Jenny had heard it was levelled after a quick sale, but here it was in front of her, a house so damaged by hard use that even at night she could see the water stains across the stucco exterior. The front door was missing, for Lerner had stacked concrete blocks in the living room and set the door flat across them to act as a bar.

Jenny moved across the lawn towards the empty doorway. The house pulsed with bass. It could have been any album, but she knew it was probably Deep Purple. Yes, of course it was. What else? She knew the song. 'Speed King'.

She stepped into the black hole doorway. To her right, the living room was locked as it was always locked when a party was going on—to give Lerner, Joey, and friends that necessary moment of preparation if a neighbour called the cops. She knocked on the living room door, even though knocking during 'Speed King' was a useless enterprise; the entirety of side one would play before anybody in the living room could hear. She moved through the little hall past the wall telephone—its cord snipped against phoned complaints regarding bass-driven high-fidelity rock—and into Lerner's kitchen. As ever, the drain board was covered with a jumble of dirty cups and TV dinner boxes picturing pork chops and applesauce. Here was the sweaty stain on the ceiling over the stove, there the seedy sofa jammed into the breakfast nook. Empty bottles stood on the stovetop—Baby Duck, Kelowna Muscatel, and Villa Berry Blend—and a dozen brown stubbies were placed in a parade behind the sink. She remembered Lerner explaining that if she could rip the Labatt's label with her thumbnail straight through, top to bottom, it meant she was a virgin. She could smell sour milk from the last time the fridge had been opened.

The door to the back deck stood open, and a quick movement outside drew her out through the door. But here she found only aluminum-framed deck chairs, much frayed, and a few terracotta pots planted with stubbed-out cigarette ends.

A door slammed somewhere inside the house, and a second later Lerner appeared in the kitchen. He opened his arms wide. "Jenny! Has our best pal left us alone again?"

"Will you go and find him for me?" she asked. "Where is he?"

"Girl, the answer is known. So we'll wait."

Lerner wrapped his arm around her shoulder, led her to the sofa, and cosied her down beside him. Lerner suited this house. He always smelled of his jacket, a brown waxed canvas that he boasted never needed cleaning. "You can't clean it," he'd told her. "It's like a salad bowl or an iron frying pan." The jacket smelled bad, although to hear him tell it, the odour did him chemical favours with the girls. It did him none with Jenny.

She wished she'd never kissed him.

Lerner said, "Relax, can't you? Sometimes you act like you've got a stick of primness up your rear."

"If Joey's here, get him. I need to talk to him." She removed his hand from her knee. "Please."

"Prim and so polite. How can I not bow to your every unreasonable womanly demand?" He hauled himself up and ambled out of the kitchen towards the living room. On impulse, she darted after him into the hallway, but the living room door shut in her face and the lock clicked. She put her ear to the door and heard a burst of laughter, but she couldn't make out Joey's laugh. Somebody put on side two of *Deep Purple in Rock*. Noise was better than quiet. Silence was a bad sign.

The door opened again, music thudding, just long enough to let Lerner through. He backed Jenny into the kitchen and held out a green glass tumbler filled with something dark. All the shadows in the room seemed to converge on it. "Joey said to drink this."

"What is it?" she asked. She'd stopped drinking beer at Lerner's house after the kissing incident. "I only drink cola."

"This too is known. What else would it be?"

A shadow crossed the deck outside the kitchen.

"Who's that?" Lerner asked, still holding the drink.

"Just Jenny's friend, looking for the gala celebration, spoils, and drink." Moira stepped inside the kitchen door and turned her green-grape eyes towards the sink, the bottles, and the stain on the ceiling. When her gaze settled on Lerner, he pulled his waxed jacket closer around himself and stood a little taller.

"I don't call this much of a party." Moira wrinkled her nose and threw herself into the sofa beside Jenny. She asked, "Is this lug the best you could do?"

"Yes," Lerner answered.

"Haven't you found your fellow, Jenny?"

"No," Jenny said. "I keep asking Lerner to get him. The door is locked."

"Break it down," Moira suggested to Lerner. "Bring the fellow out on your shoulders wearing wreaths in his hair, and place him before Jenny on his knees."

Lerner laughed aloud. "He'd eat my liver."

"Tasty. What's this?" Moira reached for the glass in Lerner's hand.

Lerner shrugged and gave it to her. "Smells like rum."

"God. You'd think men had never heard of gin." Moira drank a mouthful and grimaced. "Fine-grade motor oil."

"You're a picky one," Lerner said. "How'd you get so feminine?"

"Born with it, I guess. This place stinks. We girls will be outside. Wash a few dishes, and then we'll see whether this dump is worth our return." Moira, drink in hand, motioned Jenny ahead of her through the door onto Lerner's back deck. Overhead, the moon had come out, and its light brightened the tips of the trees on the encircling slopes.

Moira was dressed as lightly as Jenny but appeared not to notice the cold. She leaned her elbows on the deck rail, the glass between her hands, and sipped at Jenny's drink.

Jenny watched. "Does it taste like plain cola?"

Moira held the glass up and looked at Jenny through it. Light from the moon and Lerner's kitchen window reflected in the glass.

"Give me some." Jenny held out her hand. "Then I'm going back in."

"Well, this is a very funny-tasting drink. I think you should leave it alone."

"I drink cola. And I drive us home." Except for the night that Joey drove them, and crashed the Zed, and died. A night at Lerner's, very much like this impossible party, almost identical in every way — including 'Speed King' — except that Moira was with her, holding the drink that looked exactly like the one Joey had made for her, here at Lerner's party, the night he died.

"This ain't cola, sister." Moira clicked her tongue. "Well, you're not the first girl whose fellow slipped her a mickey. Or whatever this is ..." Moira emptied the glass over the rail and looked over her shoulder at the trees lining Lerner's yard. "Do you hear that?"

"Wind in the trees. It's cold. I'm going back inside."

"I know what wind sounds like, and that's not it," Moira stated. "Somebody's breathing nearby. Watching us. Well, sister, that's just one more good reason to beat our feet to a hasty retreat from this so-called party. I'll take you to a do where men don't smell like bivouac tents, and drinks smell like sugar and come in clean glasses."

"I can't leave. Joey's here, and either he'll come out of the living room soon or the record will end and I'll start pounding on the door."

"What fun you have at your parties! But too late for that. Look behind you."

Jenny turned. Where Lerner's house had stood moments before lay a roughly cleared foundation and a heap of demolition detritus. She could make out the full length of the street now, and under the trees, the Datsun 240Z.

She dug a hand into her shorts pocket for the car keys, pulled them out, and turned towards the Zed.

Moira caught a fistful of Jenny's T-shirt. "Your fellow is a washout. Now, we're going to find mine."

"Joey's in the car." With Lerner's place now an empty lot, where else would Joey be? He often left her alone in Lerner's kitchen, but he'd never drive away from the party house without her. "I'll show you."

Jenny ran across the empty lawn and along the moonlit street with Moira at her heels. She opened the driver's door and they peered inside.

Moira said, "He's not here. Unless he's curled up in the ashtray. Look, I've been patient. I've been understanding. And now I've had sufficient of your selfish behaviour."

Jenny looked up and down the empty street. She'd go door to door and wake up the neighbourhood if she had to. "Moira, this is my chance to find him. It's a matter of life or death."

"Well, maybe it is for me, too." Moira pinched Jenny's arm.

Jenny pulled herself free and said what she knew she should not. "Life or death? For you, I think that ship has sailed."

Moira set both fists on her hips. "What's that supposed to mean?"

"It seems obvious to me that you are already . . ." She stopped herself before she could say the final word.

"I'm already *leaving,* is what I am. Because neither of our fellows is here. And I'm not taking you with me, chum."

Moira's flowered skirts swirled in the wind, and then became the wind. Jenny was caught in the current, spun round and drawn off the road, upwards, as if by her collar. The stars retreated into darkness. The air blew cold and then warm against her skin. She reached her hands out, arched her back, and flew, like Wendy over Neverland.

Chapter 11

The campers were chomping their sandwiches and tossing the crusts into the long grass beside the Cove road when Jenny rejoined the hike. Malcolm must have looked away from the trail out of the woods as she arrived, because one moment there was no Jenny, and the next there she was, at the bend in the road. She stood so still that she looked like a photograph of herself: arms held outwards as if she were landing after a period of weightlessness beyond gravity's pull. So like a photograph this first glance was, that Jenny appeared overexposed, with a white flash just over her left shoulder. The line of her breast took him, as did her slender legs and the way she stood a little off-balance, so that he wanted to catch her before she fell.

A large black car tore around the bend. Malcolm stretched out his arm to prevent the boys at his back from stepping out into the car's path, so he didn't see the actual moment of impact. Malcolm heard the boys' shouts. He might have shouted as well, without knowing it.

The car knocked Jenny down. Her legs folded under her and she fell onto the gravel verge. He registered her body whole and unbroken. Terror was replaced by a steadying rage. What a bastard, Nixon kind of car, this black Eldorado, drawn up cockskew with its nose in the gravel and its tail across the road. There was a T-shirted jerk-of-the-world climbing out the driver's side.

The driver bent over Jenny. "Did I hit you?"

"Bastard." Malcolm said to the driver. "Criminal."

"She was in the road," the T-shirted man said, which was a barefaced lie.

Malcolm meant to take some kind of relevant action, but Tanaka and Flash took him by the shirt and pulled him backwards. His anger cooled slightly. Jenny hadn't been sent flying. She wasn't broken. She was sitting upright in the shadow of the Eldorado. He pulled himself together and crouched down between Jenny and the bastard driver of the car. The little yellow-shirted boys gathered closely around them, buzzing with interest and delight.

Jenny said, "I'm all right, sort of, except for being stupid."

The kids laughed, because kids loved it if you said you were stupid and confirmed what they thought.

Malcolm wanted to touch her to make sure she was real. "I thought you were hit."

"Just a bit."

"I thought you were dead."

"What, not dead?" Adrian joined them, back from the woods and cool as water. "He's always so worried about everybody, our sweet Malcolm."

Malcolm put his hand in his pocket and made a fist.

Jenny turned to the driver. "You hardly touched me."

The driver looked at his watch. "There's a ferry soon. I'll take you to the hospital."

Malcolm was not about to let Jenny go anywhere in that Eldorado. He'd fight the bastard if he had to.

But Jenny shook her head. "I don't want my cousin to know. She'd be on my case forever. I'm not hurt. Just go."

Her shorts had crept up her thighs as she sat, and Malcolm could see a long dark bruise that ran from her knee up into the bell of her shorts. "You are hurt. Don't say you're not hurt when you're hurt."

Jenny sent Malcolm a look that made him stand up and take a step back. Meanwhile, the driver had pulled out a Bic pen and was looking about him. Flash stepped forward and held out the palm of his hand. The driver scribbled something on Flash's palm, then got into the black Eldorado, backed slowly onto the road, and drove off towards Snug Cove.

The dust from the departed Eldorado settled. Malcolm crouched down beside Jenny at the side of the road. "Why didn't you see that car? Why did you let that bastard hit you?"

Jenny shook her head. "I don't know what happened. Anyway, look at this."

The dark bruise on her thigh had already faded to a shadow.

"Must have been a trick of the light," Jenny said.

Malcolm stood up. Wrong again. If he had so misjudged Jenny's injury, he wondered what else in his life he might be wrong about. Maybe his parents were correct after all, and he should head back east to work for the summer in his uncle's firm. He'd end up someday with a black Eldorado and a businessman's haircut, like that bastard who'd driven off around the bend towards the cove. Or maybe he should grant his parents' so-called secret wish for him and enlist in medical school. Perhaps he'd even underestimated Adrian, and Adrian was actually a prince among friends.

Malcolm turned to the campers. They stared back at him with surprising and appropriate solemnity.

He said, "You see, that's why I keep telling you to stay off the road."

Tanaka asked, "Can we go to the store? Adrian said we could."

"Adrian's full of ... No, you can't." Malcolm picked up a handful of gravel from the side of the road and threw it at the white everlasting across the way.

Adrian asked, "What's happened to our Ketchup?"

"He's here somewhere." Malcolm began counting campers. Once he'd caught up with them on the path through the woods, they'd walked with him all the way, and no matter how full of energy or loud of singing voice, he'd not allowed one out of his sight. "Look, I know you think I'm a loser ..."

"... and alone in your heart." Adrian laid one hand across his own breast.

"But I do take care of the kids." The campers jostled and jimmied so that he couldn't get an accurate count. Still, he didn't find Ketchup among them.

Jenny asked, "Who's missing?"

"Ketchup," Adrian told her. He added loudly, "Let's hit the road to the cove, campers."

Malcolm said, "Maybe Ketchup ran into the woods on his own."

"Don't you know anything about kids?" Adrian shot him a hooded glance over his shoulder and turned towards the cove. "As if we didn't know where he's gone."

Malcolm led the group along the side of the road towards Snug Cove. Adrian dropped back, and Malcolm felt the snap of a pebble against the seat of his pants. He shot a warning look at Adrian, who grinned. Behind them, the line of kids curled along the gravelled edge of the road that led down to the cove. Jenny walked with the kids in the rear, where Flash and Tanaka were smacking at each other with whippy alder stems. They sang, *"Honey, you can't love six. You can't love six and still do tricks . . ."*

"Hurry up." Malcolm picked up the pace.

Adrian stepped on the back of Malcolm's shoe. "I swear if people used the power of worrying for good and not just nagging, cancer would be cured by now. Ketchup is fine."

Malcolm tugged his shoe back on. "Kids get hurt all the time. Saying he's fine doesn't make it true."

"What was the name of that test, that atomic test that was supposed to kill us all?"

"Amchitka." On the day that the west coast of North America was rumoured to be sunk by that particular atomic blast, Malcolm had stuffed a pack with a change of clothes and the Narnia books in preparation for the tsunami that was supposed to rise up out of the testing zone. It didn't, and as he unpacked he'd experienced a moment of disappointment that he wasn't a refugee hero in a blasted world, leading legions of people to safety in a new green land.

Adrian said, "Yeah, Amchitka. And we're still alive."

"Still alive so far."

"In my opinion, every fear should be treated as a false alarm."

"It's a good thing you're not in charge of species survival." They approached the top of the hill that led down to Snug Cove. "Flash, Tanaka, move off the road. Can't you hear that car coming? Damn it, how do any kids survive to maturity?"

"People should be like frogs," Adrian said. Another car swooped past the line of campers towards the cove. "Everybody should have hundreds of offspring so that the lucky one or two will outlive all Malcolm Lee's collected dangers to continue the species. Look, haven't you heard of Occam's razor, you damned science student?"

The simplest solution is the right one. But there must be exceptions, or else how did you explain the complex workings of cell reproduction, or the mysteries of Jenny Riley? Over his shoulder Malcolm saw that Jenny had made her way up to the middle of the line of campers.

"Slow the hell down," Adrian groused.

"Adrian said *hell,*" one of the boys shouted. "Hell, hell, hell and *dammit.*"

"Oh, go ahead and swear," Malcolm grunted. The *hell* with them all. They had still not found Ketchup. Again Malcolm picked up speed. And in that moment, as the long wheat grass at the side of the road hissed against his shoes, he understood that he had somehow developed a reliable if unwelcome instinct. Perhaps he'd been developing it all his life, honing it on his nearly constant worry about other people. This gift, this unique talent, had come to maturity on this particular afternoon, and in this emergency. For he was certain now that Ketchup was injured. At least, he had to hope that the boy was injured, for if he were not, then Ketchup was dead. It would be one or the other. He was sure of it.

Now he sprinted towards the cove, and the campers' footsteps sped up behind him.

"*Honey, you can't love seven,*" Elvis sang out behind him, and Flash and Tanaka bellowed back, "*You can't love seven and go to heaven . . .*"

At the head of the column, pounding down the hill, Malcolm had a panoramic view of Snug Cove.

The place ought to have been in an uproar. An injured child would raise the roof of a quiet place like this. Did the island even have a doctor?

But Ketchup was small and might be lying anywhere among the sun-baked line of cars waiting for the ferry. It was up to Malcolm to find him and save him. It wouldn't be easy, because now the ferryboat was sliding across the shining bay to the dock. Car doors began to slam in the queue that led up past the general store and across Miller Road. *The general store.* Maybe Adrian was right about where Ketchup would be found. *Dead or alive,* Malcolm's brain chanted, and his runners slapped the blacktop in rhythm. *Dead or …*

Malcolm staggered to a stop as Adrian slung his arm around his neck and brought him to a halt. Adrian murmured into his ear, "Do you see any dead children? No, you see a line-up for the next ferry, which we now witness pulling into the dock. You can see here in the cove nothing more dire than the gala row of brightly dressed passengers at the ferry railing. I like the girl in the flowered dress, up there on the Sunshine Deck with her skirt flapping. Now turn and look a little to the left, where Ketchup's going to walk out of the store."

"You are such an ass." Malcolm squinted at the line of cars, scanning for Ketchup's yellow shirt. Flash and Tanaka, followed by the rest of the line, caught up with them.

"Malcolm said *ass*," Flash observed.

"We can say the f-word, then." Tanaka kicked a rock into the middle of the road. It hit a car in the queue, and the driver swore at them. "See? Everybody says it."

Malcolm was certain that the kid was lying in the parking lot behind a car, unnoticed but injured, and something large — probably some don't-give-a-damn pickup truck — was going to back over him.

Jenny ran up behind them. She said, "Look."

Ketchup strutted out of the general store doorway. He clutched a big yellow bag of chips against his middle.

Malcolm shook himself free of Adrian's arm and ran downhill alongside the queue of cars, the patter of feet behind him.

"He has his independence and chips, Malcolm," Adrian called. "If there are candy lips in his back pocket, he'll have achieved all that childhood could ask."

Malcolm ran towards Ketchup. From the rear, Flash and Tanaka shouted, "Give us some of those chips," and in the same second the ferry hooted.

The black Eldorado drove by them — the same bastard who'd hit Jenny — and he had the nerve, he had the *balls*, to wave at them as he headed towards the ferry.

Good riddance, Malcolm told him silently. *Leave this island. Never return.* But the Eldorado swooped outside the ferry line-up lane, veered right, and bumped and wallowed into the general store parking lot. That same damn Eldorado, travelling faster than it should. And that same damn screech that set Malcolm running faster than before.

Looking very small among the cars in the parking lot, with the Eldorado heading straight for him, Ketchup shoved his fist into the bag and pushed a handful of chips into his mouth. His smile was glorious.

§

In Issue 35, Jenny Riley moves in increasingly perilous circles around and inside the ghost world in her attempts to return her true love to the land of the living.

The casting call is murder

COMING SOON FROM

PULP LITERATURE PRESS

COMPLICATED GRIEF

Alex Kitt

Alex Kitt is a writer and poet who was born in Red Deer, Alberta. He now lives in Vancouver where he is completing his BFA in Creative Writing at the University of British Columbia. His work can be found in White Wall Review, Lida Literary Magazine, NōD Magazine, *and* UBC's Writing in the Time of COVID *anthology.*

COMPLICATED GRIEF

the dead inside me
when slow clouds gather
get excited
for storm.

i pretend my eyes are
prairie birds even though
they are my
father's.

i've written this poem before.

A GENTLEMAN'S PRIMER FOR WINNING DEBATES WITH YOUR FRIENDS AND ENEMIES

Mitchell Shanklin

Mitchell Shanklin lives in Seattle and enjoys writing stories with either magic or made-up science or both. In his free time he plays video, board, and mind games, reads, hikes, and has rambling philosophical arguments. (No, not all at the same time. Yet.) He is a proud member of Team Arsenic, the Dreamcrashers, the bisexual community, and Write of Passage. You can find him online at mitchellshanklin.com.

A Gentleman's Primer for Winning Debates with Your Friends and Enemies

While others might advise you to train in rhetoric or logic, I maintain that the surest and quickest way to obtain victory over your debate partner is to steal the words from their mouth and hide them away.

First, you must craft the inverse of their argument. An inverse argument should invoke confusion, anger, and perhaps a dash of fear in the heart of your opponent. Conjure as many other emotions in as many different organs as you can manage. Ideally, their response should only involve emotions that originate below the neck; those of the liver or kidneys can be especially potent. If you are certain that your opponent possesses their original appendix, this is an excellent avenue of attack.

Search for concepts which rhyme with those employed by your opponent (both semantically and syntactically) but which are off-kilter, non-isomorphic. Disharmonic. For example, if they argue that it is heartless to withhold food from the starving, you might posit that rich foods can cause great damage to the human heart.

Second, you must whisper these words within the range of their subconscious hearing. This fluctuates throughout the day based on the amount of ambient astral radiation. If your area has few nearby ley lines, at noon on a clear day, place yourself no closer than twenty but no further than thirty feet away from your opponent. A whisper just loud enough to accidentally awake a sleeping babe should do the trick. Adjust your distance and volume as needed based on the local climate.

Third, you must wait for their argument and its inverse to combine, to ferment and gestate. The average gestation period is two weeks, but there is a high degree of variance. Look for your opponent to develop especially chapped lips, or to randomly burst into song less often than they normally do. You will be able to tell that birth is imminent when the keening starts. It is impossible to miss——the elongated jaw, the silent, involuntary screams which send dogs and other pets running into the night.

Fourth, you must catch the argument-child. A net of fine-woven silver is traditional, but any metal which is resistant to corrosion will do. Be careful here. If your opponent catches sight of you with the net before the eruption is imminent, they may become wroth.

Now, others would recommend burning or beheading the child, or perhaps exposing it to the elements. Never do this. Martyrdom is a gift. If the argument-child is sufficiently mature and developed, made of flesh and song rather than mist and murmurs, you might try to absorb it. This is the surest route to victory, for not only will your opponent be unable to recall their thesis, you will be able to twist it against them at will.

The entirety of the child must enter you within a single swallow. Remember that the appropriate analogue for this process is not consumption but reverse-birth. Your mouth must be as the angry womb which seeks to reclaim what it has given to the world, that knows that it was released too early. Let the child dissolve back into its component parts within you so that you may integrate the contradiction.

If the child is not mature enough to be re-integrated, there are a variety of suitable storage mechanisms. No special security is required. While argument-children are known to smile prettily or, on occasion, to mutter snatches of sonnets, they have no true will and cannot escape of their own volition. I prefer to use small jewellery boxes.

Be gracious in your victory. Allow your opponent's tears to fall where they may. Offer a single chuckle, a pat on the back as their throat distends in horror at the loss of a deeply cherished belief.

It is meet for me to here acknowledge my own opponents. They claim that the purpose of debate is to shed light, that the goal is not to seek victory but to narrow and purify the scope of disagreement, to elevate the discourse. They would encourage you to spurn these tried and true techniques I have so gracefully shared. My reply is that a true gentleman would never posit an opinion lacking merit and that discourse is inherently a violent affair.

If any of these hooligans accost or accuse you, dear reader, do not feel obliged to raise your own net on my behalf. Instead, please write to me at your earliest convenience. You might also choose to remind them of their colleagues who, when the topic of debate etiquette is raised, turn pale and clutch at their spasming throats.

Inform them that my commitment is undiminished, that I oil and polish my net of silver each and every fortnight.

CLOTHESLINE

Kimberley Aslett

Kimberley Aslett *is a medical librarian from Northern Ontario. She's new to writing, encouraged by a mid-life community evening class and the delight of making stories after a lifetime of reading them indiscriminately. She's previously had five contest entries appear in print: two in* The Leaf, *and one each in* Canadian Stories *and the Polar Expressions Anthology. Kimberley's story 'The echo of light footsteps on parchment' (Issue 33) earned an honourable mention for the 2021 Bumblebee Flash Fiction Contest, and 'Clothesline' earned the same honours for the 2021 Hummingbird Flash Fiction Prize.*

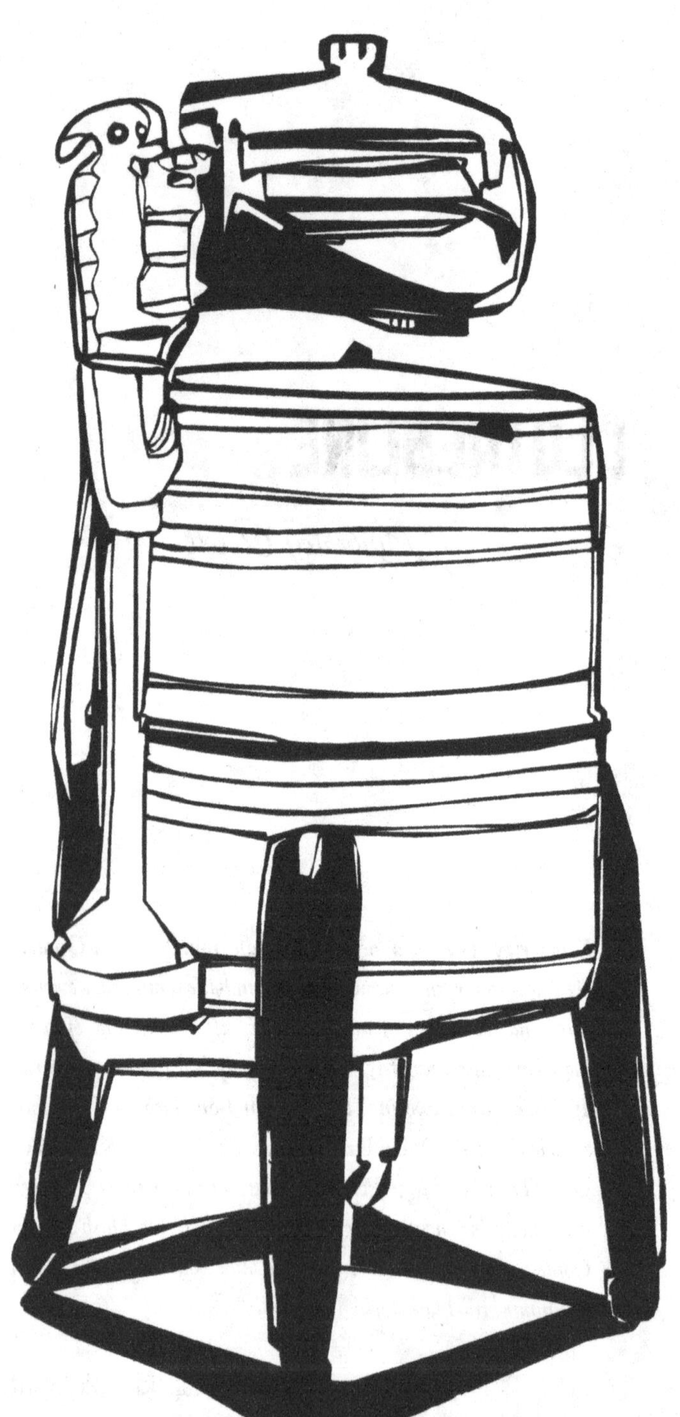

Clothesline

Reach into the laundry basket. Grasp an edge of fabric, a selvage or seam. Pull it from the hard, cold, twist of all of the other towels. It will hold the shape the wringer washer forced it into. Tease out the edge. When you've got two corners, give it a snap. Not a shake or a wiggle. The very best is a hard snap that forces all the twists out in a noise that startles the old cat right off the step or the birds into the air. Grab two clothespins from the cloth bag that is faded and has a hanger poking through one corner. One corner, pin, next corner, next towel overlapping, next pin. From the clothesline step, you see the back field, weeds dry and green-grey in the low morning sun.

This task is the one you can sense and smell so strongly it will come back to you in dreams and in hypnosis years later, when other memories have tangled up at the sides and fallen away or faded. The memory is so deep it feels like a hard nut at your centre, the same centre that doesn't want to relax in the yoga classes where you hear the chatter from your own brain in every silent moment. The centre that won't give up its tears and pain in the expensive therapy.

You were five. Or seven. You had to reach to put the towels up there. It was a big help, she told you. You felt like you were doing a complicated dance.

The towels were used hard over the years. They lost colour, became a similar yellow-grey, no matter the bleach or soap. They were used until they got holes, then they were cut into rags. Sometimes the rags got stained with grease or blood. Your mother would rinse the bloodied rags separately to get out the stains, her head down over a small pail in the kitchen sink.

Your family left that house, and the place that was rented after that had no clothesline, only a dryer. The dryer was in the basement where you could retreat from the sounds of your father's boots coming in from working in the yard, greasy and sweaty and strong. If you were alone in the house, you would wait until he left to go back out before getting a sandwich. Sometimes you could play the cassette player to drown out the noises from upstairs.

Sometimes, as you went from child to adult, you found yourself touching the clothes that came out of the washer, flat and stiff. You wished you needed to untangle these, smooth them, make them absorb the sun and the smell of outside. But your jeans were too stiff for a clothesline, and the dryer made it easier to escape into your room with a book.

You lived in apartments where you could hang your clothes on hangers to dry at the windows when you didn't have the money for the coin dryer or when it was a sheer top for the bar on Saturday night. But mostly you constructed a careful life, finished school, found a partner, did those things. You managed to look like you were living in it instead of trying to fake normal, instead of watching to see how to be like other girls.

When you had your baby, you hung cloth diapers and blankets on your own clothesline at the old house you two, and now three, rented. The diapers were stiff when they dried, but the baby was never happy anyway. You were tired and worried, and you had dreams of the baby falling. You switched to disposables for the second baby. Your partner said it didn't matter, it was OK if that was what you wanted.

Once, you cut your hand on a glass in the sink and wrapped a tea towel around it while you found the bandages and got the salt from the pantry. When you had cleaned up the cut, you filled a pail with salt water, and when you shook the towel open, the sight of the blood against the white cotton with the blue trim made you cry. You hung it to dry on the line later.

PULP
Literature
JJ Lee
'The Man in the
Long Black Coat'

PULP
Literature
Carol Berg
'Uncanonical Murder'

PULP
Literature
Matthew Hughes
'The Devil You Don't'
Mel Anastasiou
Carolyn Oliver
Eric Del Carlo
TJ Berg
Axel Raikis
Allaigna's Song: Aria

PULP
Literature
George McWhirter
'Stalk'

Allaigna's Song
Overture
J M Landels

PULP
Literature

FANTASTIC
FRESH
FICTION

www.pulpliterature.com

ARS POETICA

Mitchell Bodo

Mitchell Bodo is a poet from Hamilton, Ontario. He earned a Bachelor of Arts (Honours) in English Literature, graduating *summa cum laude* from McMaster University. His writing process is as follows: he gets sad, then writes it down.

Ars Poetica

Cos tonight we're celebrating that I am
Not dead that Lulu didn't eat my last joint
And I do not have to rush her to the hospital

Yes, I am guilty of sometimes being ironic
I'm twenty-two now and still can't picture
What it's like to feel earnestly about anything

It's not that I don't enjoy the touch
Of a windowpane bathed in sunlight
Or laughing hysterically at harmless

Displays of human stupidity but my stomach aches
For a burrito and there are patches of time
Where I look up into the sky and squint like when

My brother held up an entire funeral procession
Because he had to pee he was only one of
The pallbearers — don't feel bad about it Brock

Papa would've found that shit hilarious although
I have no idea what to make of it or the years that
Followed I can only roll my eyes and say *whatever,*

Whatever, whatever. It's hard to find meaning
In a world that isn't predicated on your existence
Like, at all, but I still spend hours picking

My fingernails and contemplating emptiness.
I am the crash dummy of such existential
Conundrums the bearer of keys that open doors

To nowhere, let time morph me like an
Aging movie reel, let me fade like frames
Of celluloid baking in the open sun.

Drop a grand piano on my forehead
I'll slink all the way home.

WOULD WE HAD TIME

Lorina Stephens

Lorina Stephens has worked all sides of the publishing desk since 1980, and for twelve years operated Five Rivers Publishing as a house which gave voice to Canadian authors. Due to life circumstances, she had to change direction, and so now the house exists as a bit of a vanity press for her work. Her short fiction has appeared in literary and genre publications such as On Spec, Polar Borealis, Postscripts to Darkness, *and* Neo-Opsis. *She also co-edited, with Susan MacGregor,* Tesseracts 22: Alchemy and Artifacts. *When not writing or gardening, she is a watercolour artist who lives with her husband of forty-plus years in a 150-year-old stone house in a tiny village in mid-Western Ontario. You can find her at fiveriverspublishing.com, and on Facebook at facebook.com/ FiveRiversPublishing.*

Would We Had Time

Although it's one of many he's made, this chronometer feels heavy. There is a weight to it which has nothing to do with science or logic, nothing to do with the precision, eight-day movement, the spring-detent escapement. *Arnold 294.* He writes that designation in his inventory, noting it's been purchased by the British Royal Navy.

Time and time and time is what he makes, the recording of it, the marking of it, even the fabrication of it, he thinks. He wonders would we even be aware of time were it not for these machines, these values we have placed upon the movement of the sun, the dividing of our days. What if he were to stop making clocks altogether? Perhaps the memory of time might slip away, and we'd forget about placing ourselves in peril in the pursuit of the terrifying unknown.

Apparently this one's to be assigned to the *Erebus,* which is now under command of Sir John Franklin and headed for the Arctic.

He settles it into its box, French-fitted and lined with baize.

He looks over to its twin on his workbench, not yet numbered. He tries to brush off his sense of doom. It's that he's tired, he is sure: long hours, little sleep, need for a meal and his bed and a few hours respite.

"Mr Young, if you please," he yells, and his apprentice ducks in. "Take this to the quartermaster's office at Navy Hall. Right smart about it." And he closes the lid on the box, fixes the brass latch, and pushes it across his bench.

He feels the weight of the timepiece in his hand, knows it well: *Arnold 294*, the impossibility of it fifteen years gone.

He looks up at the relic of a man before him, feels the weight of *that* knowledge.

"Mr Young. How?"

"You know me, sir?"

"Only just." He gestures to the chronometer. "How?" Looking at the man before him, he remembers the young apprentice, only eighteen, and the apology written in haste:

Signed on to Erebus. My deepest apologies, Sir, for my failure of faith, and my eternal gratitude for yours.

"Why?"

Young leans heavily on the counter, seeming to fall into a swoon. Arnold ducks around, takes the boy — the boy; surely a man now — under the arm and leads him to the back room where he settles him into a chair, pours him brandy. "Shall I fetch the doctor?"

Young swallows the brandy, gasps, and waves it off. "No. No more. No doctor. Sir, I need your help." And the creature breaks down, cradling his head in his hands, his sobs wracking that frail frame. "What I have seen. What I have done. God help me. The chronometer! Where is it?" The boy makes to rise, falls back, holding his head.

Arnold hastily fetches the chronometer — it feels so heavy — and places it in Young's hands. He's locked the door, turned the sign, spoken a word through the other door to the workshop that he's not to be disturbed under any circumstances. His staff, he knows, can be relied upon.

"I have a story to tell you," Young says at length, "one which I owe, God help me. And when I have done, I beg you take this damned thing from me and get rid of it. I'm going to die, sir, and I am sorry to burden you with my troubles, but please, I beg you have me buried in sacred ground. Sacred ground, I beg you."

"Calm, Mr Young. Calm. I am your friend, ever was."

Young looks up at him, those sunken eyes wet with weeping, pain and horror in the premature lines of that young face. The boy gathers a breath, another, slowing himself, collecting his reserves which seem scant at best, and then in the privacy of Arnold's room reveals the events of the past fifteen years, how he'd been captivated by the romance and lure of an Arctic exploration, that here was a chance for him to make himself, the apprentice horologist become explorer. It was the stuff of legend. And he could care for the all-important chronometer, upon which so much of ship navigation depended.

There had been exhilaration in the first weeks of May, entering Baffin Bay in August 1845, signalling a hello to whalers. Cold. Pack ice coming down a week after. The week after that, thicker yet. But all would be well. They were surely only days from finding the Northwest Passage. Men fell sick from bad tinned food. The compass was unstable. The chronometer was unable to assist in an accurate reading as a result. No one said it, but everyone thought it: lost. Here there be dragons. And the cold—the invasive, persistent, deep cold.

And now the crew sank into despair. Their rations were gone but they were too weak to find, fish, forage, or hunt for food.

Hardtack and lemon juice, an ache in the limbs, and headaches were common. But onward until just like that, both *Erebus* and *Terror* part of the ice, an endless, relentless sheet of ice where no man nor beast was to be found.

But ever the chronometer kept the time, if the compass did not keep the direction. Three years of that. Three years and then ships abandoned, a hopeless trek to find Back's Fish River.

"I kept the chronometer for Captain Crozier." Young takes a shuddering breath. "Even after I lost them in the freezing fog. It was the Copper tribe found and took me in." He looks up at Arnold, those blue eyes lost to colour—vacant, grey, and haunted.

"And how do you come to be back home?"

"Bay traders. The Copper wanted shot of me, sent me off with their furs. I don't know why the traders agreed." He shrugs. "From there sledded south. They didn't discover the chronometer. I hid it on my person. I let it wind down, feared for the marking of time, feared for its discovery which could mean my death either through murder and robbery or abandonment, or hanging should I ever make it home." He gulps in air. "Made my way as ship's boy when finally we made Montreal.

"But it's no good, Mr Arnold. I cannot make my way. Every limb is painful, and my head constantly a misery. I am done for. And the one thing I could sell and allow myself a way forward is the one thing I dare not. So I come to you. Because I know you are a fair man, or at least were. And I am dying. I know it." He gestures to the brass chronometer, which is well-worn and shining despite its long journey. "I turned my back on the making of time, and so time has had her vengeance.

"If I could sleep here tonight, sir? Someplace safe. Someplace familiar. I won't burden you beyond what I asked of you."

And how could a decent man deny? Arnold took the boy to the couch in the office, settled him with a coat tucked over him, thought to send for a pie but then not. Best let the boy sleep. Then the shuddering gasp. One moment a man is here. Then next, not.

The chronometer, *Arnold 294*, he took to his workbench and set to altering it. It would make a handsome carriage clock. There were buyers for such things. And there were ways to bring a man peace. Would we had time to do better.

PULP
Literature
Good books for the price of a beer
Allaigna's Song Overture JM Landels
PULP Literature
Short stories, poetry, and comics you can't put down
www.pulpliterature.com

THE REALM OF SHADOWS

Megan W Shaw

Megan W Shaw lives near Toronto with her partner and one-and-a-half-year-old daughter. She is an emerging writer and the founder of Leading Word Education, a literacy enrichment charity. Her fiction can also be found in Cossmass Infinities. 'The Realm of Shadows' was an honourable mention for the 2021 Hummingbird Flash Fiction Prize

The Realm of Shadows

It is important to get there before the sun. If you are already present, already a part of the landscape, you will cause no disruptions. Wait in stillness until the sun has crested the hill and the forest accepted the end of night. Then you may walk. But move slowly, carefully. Sway as the branches and skip as the creek. Do not run unless you are swift enough to blend with the wind. Any motion unnatural to the forest will frighten them, and your chance will be lost.

Look to the shadows of the stones first. The ones that are low enough, smooth enough to rest upon. The ones that are high enough, rough enough to climb.

The trees will take longer.

Look to the shadows of those steps and boulders that dawn reveals, and speak the words of one who has passed. They must be of one who has frequented these woods, and they must be words that have meaning here.

That is when you will start to see ghosts.

It will be those of animals at first. Many frogs, squirrels, and raccoons who visited the stones before departing continue to do so after. You will see their shapes leap, crawl, and perch within the shadows. As the shadows. For that is how they visit our sphere—through the lingering night within dawn's light.

You will know the trees' shadows have awakened when you begin to catch quick flight in the corner of your eye. The birds of that realm are skittish at first and will not stretch their wings to soar until the trees have shed their grogginess.

The shadows will then welcome shapes like yours and mine— ones that conquer the space inhabited by the small. The newly arrived, returned from their slumber, will visit the stones and trees well-known to them, in the manner they did many times before. Routine is a comfort not only to the living.

Follow the paths your loved one walked in life, and visit the sites that brought them joy. Trust in and respect the sentimentality of people, and you will be trusted and respected in kind. Believe in my words. Believe in the shadows. The supernatural cannot be seen without belief.

Do not arrive at the forest with additional expectations. You won't get to embrace your loved one. You won't get to hear them speak. Shadows cannot touch; they cannot talk. But they can see and listen. Speak the words that have been harbouring in your heart, desperate for their intended. Show the love you didn't show when time was running out.

I wish you success, my child. May this knowledge help you heal, and may you share it with those in need of healing when I have passed into the realm of shadows.

THE BALANCE

Douglas Smith

Douglas Smith is a multi-award-winning Canadian author described by Library Journal as 'one of Canada's most original writers of speculative fiction'. His fiction has been published in twenty-seven languages and thirty-five countries. His books include the novel The Wolf at the End of the World, *the collections* Chimerascope *and* Impossibilia, *and the writer's guide* Playing the Short Game: How to Market & Sell Short Fiction. *His story 'The Last of a Thing' appeared in* Pulp Literature Issue 12, Autumn 2016. Doug is a three-time winner of Canada's Aurora Award and has been a finalist for the Astounding Award, CBC's Bookies Award, Canada's juried Sunburst Award, and France's juried Prix Masterton and Prix Bob Morane. His website is smithwriter.com and he tweets at twitter.com/smithwritr.

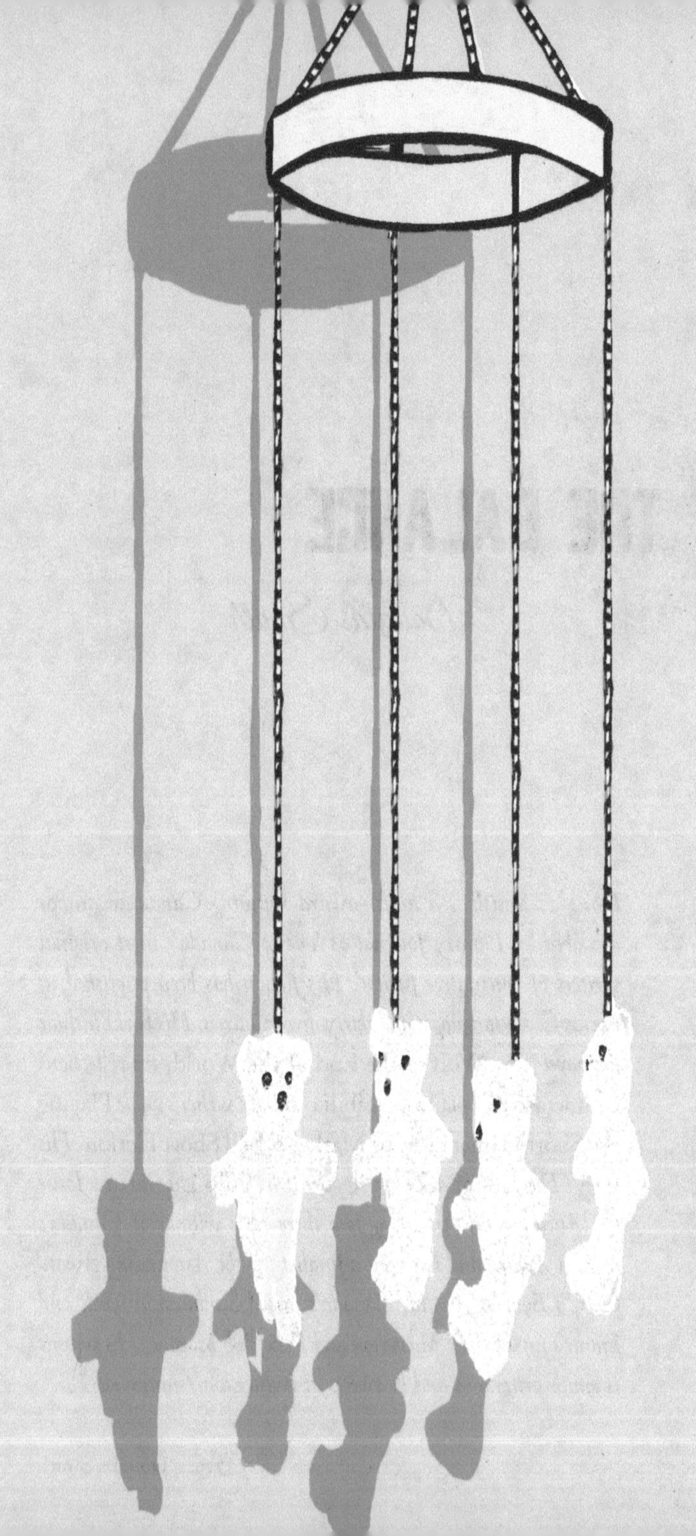

The Balance

Neon light glared off white walls and a cacophony of primary colours. Big plastic balls, a slide, toys, stuffed animals. Jack rolled over, disoriented until he remembered where he was—sleeping on a cot in a playroom at Sick Kids. The Hospital for Sick Children. Ward 4B.

A nurse stood over him. Fear grabbed Jack and pulled him awake. "What's wrong? Is Ben okay?"

The nurse smiled. "Ben's fine, Mr Fraser. He's crying, though. I think he's hungry. I checked him, and he doesn't need changing yet."

Jack struggled to focus on her. Brown hair pulled straight back from a round face and round glasses. Jennie. She was great with Ben. Hell, they were all great.

"Thanks, Jen. Be right there," he mumbled, dry-mouthed and raspy, his heart still pounding.

Jennie smiled and left. He rolled over. The cot sagged in the middle and smelled of the sweat of strangers even through the fresh sheets. He checked his phone. 2:35 am.

Groaning, he pulled on his runners, tucked his black T-shirt into his jeans, and stepped out into the darkened corridor.

Antiseptic cleaner on mopped floors fought the ubiquitous odour of medicines and soiled diapers. Ward 4B was the neurosurgery ward. Ben had been here for his two weeks of life, except for an initial stay in the neonatal ICU. Jack slept over most nights now, and would until Ben was over this recent apnea trouble.

His running shoes squeaked on the wet floor. *Apnea.* Yet another medical term he'd learned over his time here, along with *spina bifida, peritoneal shunt, compressed trachea,* and too many more. He wondered when any sort of equilibrium would return to his life.

Ahead, the nurses' station was an island of light. His gut clenched with a sudden jab of memory.

A month before Ben had been born, Cathy's doctor told them Ben wouldn't survive the birth. Cathy had carried him that last month believing that.

But Ben *had* survived. With Cathy still in recovery, an ambulance had rushed Ben and Jack thirty miles to Sick Kids. That day, Jack stood at this same station, more alone than he'd ever felt in his life, while white-coated doctors hovered, waiting for him to sign forms he couldn't understand. Forms to allow strangers to cut open his newborn son. The pen in his hand that day felt like a dead weight, as cold and heavy as his sudden life-and-death responsibility. After, he swore never to feel that powerless again. The next time, Ben would have someone on his side, someone who understood.

Reaching the nurses' station, Jack called a 'hi' to Mary, the other nurse on shift, then turned into the room where they kept Cathy's breast milk refrigerated. Cathy was still at North York General, recovering from severe complications from the pregnancy and caesarean delivery, but she sent down her milk each day. After warming the bottle, he walked to Ben's room.

Cribs lined the walls to the left and right, like chrome-barred cages shining cold under dimmed fluorescents. Spaced along the wall opposite the door, three Isolette units sat below night-darkened windows. All the cribs were occupied, but only one of the Isolettes.

Ben had spent his initial days of life in an Isolette, enclosed in a dome of plastic, a jumble of tubes fed through the ends, side openings fitted with rubber gloves for changing and feeding. That's where Jack had first touched him, where his son's tiny hand first squeezed Jack's finger through the cool, tight gloves that left a rubber smell on his hands for hours afterwards. Unable to hold his new son, he'd sat by the Isolette that first night, stroking the tiny infant through the gloves as Ben lay sleeping inside.

Rubbing his eyes, he walked over to Ben's crib. His son was lying with his thumb in his mouth, his blue-and-white knitted blanket covering his legs. His stuffed puppy was propped up against the crib bars where he could see it. Its bright red overalls with the yellow patch set a sharp contrast to the white coats of the staff and the grey-green of the walls.

Jack lowered the side of the crib then carefully lifted Ben. Settling into the yellow wooden rocking chair that some past parents had donated, he began to feed his son.

Now was the dangerous time, the quiet time when the pace slowed, when he had time to think. To think about his fears. He looked around the room.

He hated this place. Sure, it had saved Ben's life, but he still hated the constant fear, the decisions the doctors constantly laid before him, the never-ending need to surrender his son's life to strangers.

Not that any doctor on this ward was a stranger anymore. Jack knew them all. And they knew him. The dad who had learned to read the medical charts. The dad who asked questions. The dad who was a pain in the ass.

The doctors and nurses here were incredible, but necessarily objective. Jack was anything but, which made every day a battle over what was best for Ben. But as much as he hated it here, he knew his real fear.

Decisions in the hospital were tough but clear. Understand the options, make the call, then hand the problem over to the experts.

But one day soon, the hospital would discharge Ben, and Jack and Cathy would take him home. That should have been a joyful event, something to look forward to, but it meant that he and Cathy would have to become the experts, Ben's only guides through a world not built for kids with problems.

And no doctor could tell him just what those problems might be. The extent of Ben's handicaps was still unknown. He might never walk or even sit up. He might be totally dependent on Jack and Cathy. His mental faculties might be impaired.

And Jack just didn't know if he'd be able to handle that.

So despite how much he hated the hospital, he knew it was his own Isolette, protecting him from the real world and what the future would bring.

He rocked Ben a while longer, then changed him and put him back to bed. He sat beside the crib until Ben fell asleep, then returned to the dark playroom and his cot. Unable to fall back to sleep, he put in his earbuds and hit play. As Springsteen's mournful 'Downbound Train' came on, he turned up the volume, trying to drown out his thoughts and fears.

He woke with a start, flinging out his arms as if he were falling. Morning sunlight streamed through the window. He'd fallen asleep, earbuds still in, Springsteen long silent.

The wisp of a fading dream slipped from its seat in his consciousness as he remembered that Ben's fourth operation was this morning. Pushing away his fears, he hurried to Ben's room.

Most of the kids in the room were awake. Ben lay quietly staring up at the Winnie-the-Pooh mobile over his crib.

Jack picked up Ben's chart from where it hung at the end of his crib. He noted the large 'NPO' entry — *nil per os* — nothing by mouth.

"No brekkie for you, dude," he said to Ben. "You'll have to tough it out." Not that an empty tummy compared to being cut open — again.

Picking Ben up, he sniffed. "Oh thanks, stinky. Start my day off with poopers. Well, let's get you ready for your big performance." He talked to Ben while changing him, knowing it was mostly for himself. Talking was better than thinking.

Today's procedure was an arterial sling. An artery was compressing Ben's trachea, causing him to intermittently stop breathing. The surgeon would use a stitch to sling the problem artery over a convenient bone and remove the pressure on the windpipe.

It meant putting Ben's life in the hands of strangers yet again. Even after the surgery, Ben might still need an apnea monitor until he was a year old. More problems to take home, another weight on the scales of life tipped against Ben. And Jack.

He sat rocking Ben, his emotions rising and falling with the chair, until the surgeon came with the permission forms to sign. By now, Jack knew every form, and the doctors knew they needed to discuss options and risks with him in detail and well in advance of any operation. So signing the forms was simply the last formality before he allowed strangers to slice open his son.

Jennie came in, followed by an orderly with a gurney to take Ben down for pre-op. Jennie smiled at Jack, then patted Ben's head where he lay against Jack's shoulder. "Ready for another battle, little guy?"

"He is. I'm not," Jack said.

"Hey, you've got the easy part."

Yeah, right, he thought. Jennie laid Ben on the gurney. Jack stroked his son's soft hair with a finger then kissed his forehead before the orderly wheeled Ben out of the ward. Following them to the elevator, Jack watched the doors close on his son, then sighed and turned away.

After showering, he went down to the cavernous cafeteria in the basement. No windows, ugly yellow walls, mismatched tables and chairs. And hospital food, today a choice of runny scrambled eggs with greasy bacon or undercooked pancakes.

He chose the pancakes and a seat far away from any doctors, afraid of what he might hear. He understood that doctors required a clinical detachment, but hated hearing them discuss cases as if each child were just another name on another form. And he always feared that one of the names might be Ben's.

The parents' lounge was on the first floor, just off the main entrance. The room was large, with different levels and alcoves, a high ceiling, big windows, lots of plants, and soft lighting. Worn but comfortable couches and chairs lined the walls beside tables and reading lamps.

The place was cosy enough, but Jack had spent too much time here with surgeons, agonizing over life-and-death decisions for

Ben. He knew why doctors often chose one of the small alcoves for more private talks with parents, and why the murmur of those conversations was often strained and mixed with crying.

He sank into a big armchair. He hated this part of an operation day the most—waiting, never knowing if Ben had lived or died until the surgeon finally appeared. Everyone here was waiting for a similar meeting, and dreading it too. Waiting and dreading—that summed up his hospital time. With tense discussions and arguments with doctors thrown in for variety.

He'd been there for one hour and two coffees when a stout grey-haired woman in a volunteer's blue smock walked through the lounge calling his name. He identified himself, and she walked over. Her name tag said 'Elizabeth'.

She smiled. "Mr Fraser, Ben is in recovery now."

He swallowed, his mouth dry. "How'd it go?" he asked, knowing he'd get the standard answer.

Elizabeth shook her head. "Oh, they don't tell *us* that," she replied, and he wasn't sure if she was scolding him for asking or the hospital for not confiding in volunteers. "But Dr Lewis will be down to talk to you soon." She smiled again and wished him a nice day.

Define 'nice', he thought, slumping back into his chair.

About twenty minutes later, he spotted Lewis entering the lounge. Despite telling himself he wouldn't this time, Jack still tried to read the man's face as he approached.

The arterial sling was a cardiology operation, not neurosurgery, so Lewis was new to him. Jack had met him for the first time two days ago when the surgeon explained the procedure, and Jack added yet another name to his list of doctors with control over his son's life.

Unlike the neonatal neurosurgeons, Lewis seemed uncomfortable dealing with a parent. His handshake was limp, and his eyes never quite met Jack's.

But he brought good news.

"The operation was a complete success, Mr Fraser," Lewis began, and then provided details likely coherent only to a fourth-year medical student.

But Jack didn't mind. Ben was okay. He clarified some points so he could relay the correct information to Cathy and asked when Ben would be out of recovery.

"Two hours," Lewis replied, looking around the room as if for an escape route. "We'll move him directly to NICU. He'll be there until he's stabilized."

"How long will that—" Jack began.

"Can't tell in advance," Lewis interrupted. "He'll be there at least overnight." Lewis stood up, duty done, meeting over.

Jack thanked him, then phoned Cathy with the news. Returning to the lounge, he collapsed into a chair, finally able to let go. He was shaking. Too much stress, too little sleep. How long could he handle this? He closed his eyes.

Jack startled himself awake. Around him in the lounge, a few people glanced at him then turned away.

A dream. Something familiar about it, as if he'd dreamt it before. He reached for a memory, but it slipped over the edge of recall and fell away.

He sighed. *Yeah, let's add recurring nightmares to the mix*, he thought. Yet the dream had left a remnant, not of fear, but rather of some message.

A message he couldn't remember. Or didn't want to.

After he received word that Ben was out of recovery, Jack went up to the NICU. The elevators to the wards were past the lounge, a ride with which he had become all too familiar. The elevator doors clunked open then closed behind him, and a tinny bell ticked off the floors to the NICU on the fifth.

Ben had been in the NICU for at least one night after each of his operations, so Jack knew most of the nurses here. He had high respect for the neurosurgery nurses, but the ones in the NICU were angels. He couldn't fathom how they coped with the severe cases and the higher death rate here, yet still remain friendly and upbeat. He recalled visiting his grandmother in a nursing home as a teenager, and his shock at how bitter and cynical the support staff were. More hope for the young, maybe. Still a whole lifetime ahead for these kids. *Yeah, but what kind of life?*

The NICU nurses welcomed him like an old friend, saying how much they'd missed Ben, how well he was doing, how big he'd grown, and how cute he was. Jack slipped into the required hospital gown, and a nurse named Willy—"Short for Wilhelmina. So you know why I go by Willy"—led him to the room with Ben.

Ben lay in an Isolette, eyes closed, a mask over his nose. He wore only diapers and sprouted a jungle of tubes. A large bandage covered most of his chest. His stuffed puppy stood propped up outside the unit, like a fuzzy guardian straining but failing to hold back the reality of the scene.

Jack swallowed, and his concern must have shown on his face. Willy patted his arm.

"Don't worry about all the plumbing." She started pointing at the various tubes. "The one in his mouth is to support his breathing until the trachea recovers. The mask gives him a higher concentration of oxygen. That one's the apnea monitor, and of course that's the IV."

He thanked her, and she left.

He slipped his hand into the gloves of the unit, the feel of the cool rubber taking him back to Ben's first days of life. Once again unable to hold his son, he could only stroke Ben as he lay sleeping and watch Ben's chest rise and fall, his son's fragile life barely noticeable in that tiny movement.

Jack knew Ben would not remember any of this, the hours his dad stood soothing him, watching and worrying. Well, Jack would remember. And maybe it was better that Ben would have no memory of this place or all the things they'd had to do to him to keep him alive.

"You're gonna grow up with a well-earned distrust of anyone in a white coat, buddy," he muttered.

When Willy came to change Ben's dressing, Jack saw the new incision. Raw and red, cross-hatched and Frankenstein ugly, it was longer than Ben's H-shaped abdominal incision from his initial operation, the one that had installed the shunt for his hydrocephalus. Jack's eyes traced the raised line of the shunt under Ben's skin, running down his thin neck and tiny chest to that first incision.

They'd saved his son, but they'd marked him for life. *Marked me too*, he thought.

"He's a little warrior," Willy said.

"With scars for every battle," he added, pulling his eyes away.

Jack spent the evening beside the Isolette, soothing Ben through the gloves when the infant woke, talking to him through the glass. Most of the time, Ben just slept, which was best for his recovery anyway.

Jack would have to sleep down on 4B again. The NICU had no overnight facility, and they didn't let parents sleep in the room. Too many incidents occurred, and the nurses needed quick and clear access to all the babies. The NICU would call the nurse's station at 4B if anything changed with Ben.

Willy returned as Jack was about to leave for the night. Going over to another Isolette, she lifted the cover and took out a baby boy who couldn't have weighed more than four pounds. Jack had asked Willy about him earlier. The baby had a cleft palate and internal problems, along with deformed arms.

Sitting in a rocking chair, holding the child in her arms, she began to sing softly. *"Hush, little baby, don't say a word . . ."*

"Parents been in yet?" he asked.

Willy shook her head. "Not since little Davey here was admitted a week ago. But I'll be damned if he won't know some love just because he ended up with the wrong parents," she said, not taking her eyes off the baby.

"At least they named him."

"Nope. I did. All we have from them is the last name." She looked down at the baby. "I always liked the name David."

But, he thought, *you won't have to take him home. You won't have to deal with his handicaps for the rest of your life.*

He suddenly wanted to be anywhere but in that room. He gave Ben a goodnight pat through the gloves, nodded to Willy, and left. Her lullaby followed him down the hall.

". . . and if that diamond ring don't shine, Momma's gonna buy you . . ."

And if those legs of yours don't work, he thought, *what's Daddy going to do?*

The song stayed in his head until he fell asleep thinking of faceless parents turning their backs on their children.

Jack sat straight up in bed, a premonition of something wrong and his own cry echoing in the empty room his only reminders of a fading dream.

He flung off the damp covers and jammed on his shoes. His watch showed 2:30 am. His heart pounding hard, he ran up the one flight to the fifth floor. Opening the door, he heard more noise than he should at this time of night. Loud voices and some sort of beeping. A blue light flashed in the hall. He turned the corner to the NICU.

Through the locked access door, he saw nurses running towards the last door on the left.

Ben's room.

He pounded with both palms on the reinforced glass of the door. Only one nurse, not one he knew, remained at the station. She looked up at him, startled. She just shook her head and motioned at him to go away.

"Let me in," he screamed through the glass. "My son's in that room."

The glass muffled her reply beyond understanding. He shook his head and waved towards Ben's room. The nurse did a quick scan of the life monitor readings displayed at the station, then jumped up and ran down the hall towards the room.

He closed his eyes tight. *No, no, no. God, no. Let him be okay. Just one more time, let him be okay.*

Still leaning against the door, he let his head slump forward until it bumped against the cold glass.

Just one more time, he prayed.

He stood there, staring through the glass, waiting and praying, until a nurse emerged from the room and came down the hall towards him. He couldn't remember her name, but she knew him.

She was holding both her palms up towards him in a 'calm down' motion and mouthing, "It's okay," over and over.

He felt his shoulders droop. His hands shook and his legs felt weak as tension fled his muscles, leaving adrenaline behind.

The nurse, whose name tag read 'Sally', hit the button to let him pass through the door. As he stepped inside, she raised her hands again.

"It's okay, Mr Fraser. Ben is fine."

He forced himself to take a deep breath. "Oh, god. Thank god. Sorry. I was … I mean, I saw …"

Sally nodded. "He's all right."

"What happened? What was wrong?" He started down the hall.

Sally put a hand on his arm. "I'm sorry, but you'll have to wait outside here until we come and get you."

He looked at her. "Why? What—"

"It wasn't Ben. It was … another baby."

It took a moment for him to understand her words and the expression on her face. "Oh."

Sally held the door open for him, and he stepped back out. Slumping into a chair in the hall, he watched Sally walk back to Ben's room. She wasn't walking very fast, and he was afraid he knew why.

About fifteen minutes later, Sally let him into the NICU. After donning a gown, he walked into Ben's room. His son was lying quietly awake.

In the same chair where she'd been rocking Davey, Willy sat crying. Davey's Isolette was empty. Jack put a hand on her shoulder.

"Davey?"

She nodded. "His heart stopped."

She stood up, and he gave her a hug.

"Should be used to this shit," she said, stepping back and wiping her eyes. "How can parents like that exist? He died alone."

"No. He had you."

She smiled sadly. "Shoulda had more."

"Yeah."

"Guess we gave you a scare. Sorry, Jack."

He walked over to Ben. "I thought …"

She came to stand beside him. "Sure you did."

"I was so relieved …"

"Well, of course you were. You're not like Davey's parents. Hell, I'll bet—" She stopped. "Never mind."

He looked at her. "You think they'll be glad …" He let it go unfinished.

She nodded. "Glad they don't have a *problem* anymore."

"Maybe they just didn't know if they could handle it. Day after day. All their lives," he said, almost to himself.

Willy looked at him but said nothing.

He swallowed. "Willy, sometimes I wonder if …" But he couldn't bring himself to say it.

"Ah," she said quietly. "I see."

They stood there, looking down at Ben. Finally, she spoke again. "So how many procedures has he had so far?"

"Four," Jack said, his voice barely a whisper.

"And how many times have we rousted you out of bed for an apnea episode or the like?"

He shrugged. "Lost count. A bunch."

"And how'd you feel after? When you knew he was okay? How'd you feel just now? When you knew it wasn't him?"

He thought back over all those times, thought about how he was feeling right then. "Thankful," he said quietly.

She nodded. "That's the answer to that question you've been asking yourself." She squeezed his arm. "Stop beating yourself up, Jack. You're one of the good ones."

She picked up Davey's chart. "Better get the damn paperwork over with." She left the room.

He looked at Ben lying quietly amidst a jungle of tubes. His son was scarred. He wasn't perfect. Jack and Cathy would have years, maybe a lifetime of being more than full-time parents to this child.

Yet Jack felt a strange calm for the first time since the month before Ben was born, when Cathy's doctor had told them that Ben wouldn't survive the birth. Cathy had carried him that last month believing that.

"You keep making liars out of them, don't you?" he whispered. "Well, let's just keep on doing that. You and me and Mommy."

The universe didn't work perfectly, but maybe it did care, because somehow, in that moment, he felt a balance. Something, somewhere was trying to give Ben a chance.

And Jack was part of that balance. Because he wanted to be. Because he cared, too.

He slipped a hand into one of the gloves, and gently stroked Ben's soft hair.

Willy poked her head back into the room. "Just got word. Your little guy's fully stabilized. We're transferring Ben back to 4B in the morning. Doctor Bernstein may even discharge him next week."

Bernstein was the head of neurosurgery. Jack nodded.

Willy looked at him. "So, you think he's ready for that? To go home?"

He looked down at Ben, who stared right back into his eyes. "Yeah. He's ready." Jack smiled. "We both are."

"Here's the birthday boy!" Jack calls.

With Jack holding his hands, five-year-old Ben walks to where Cathy waits on the seesaw. The playground sand makes Ben more unsteady than usual, but his new leg braces are helping. Cathy guides Ben to sit in front of her, then wraps her arms around him in a hug.

Reaching up, Jack grabs the other seat, the sun-baked wood warm under his fingers, and pulls down. Ben squeals, and Cathy laughs as they lift into the air.

Jack swings a leg over and settles into the other seat. He gives a gentle push, and they rise and fall, rise and fall, the three of them, together and in perfect balance.

SELF DOUBT WITH AUTEBEUF

Derek Webster

Derek Webster's book Mockingbird was a finalist for the 2016 Gerald Lampert Award for best poetry debut. He received an MFA from Washington University in St Louis and is the founding editor of Maisonneuve magazine. His poetry and prose have appeared in many publications, including The Malahat Review, The New Quarterly, Boston Review, The Walrus, and elsewhere. He lives in Montreal.

Self-Doubt with Rutebeuf

The wind lifted
                blew
     me back
to a corner of your field
            where I grew
        to awkward height——

                If you seek
     my gnarled limbs,
             you'll become
          master of all
             your little bum spies

        until
     winter comes to strip
your world

     I am all that's left
           my appetites
     don't rest——

King

of cheap rent

poor man's

glory

I am the soiled arm

of self-doubt

reaching

miles deep

into your eyes
to mineralize
your name.

If you were smart
you'd leave me to wizen

upon life's brown plain —

Sad
rutabaga, it's you

forever

on the threshold

inviting me in.

RESPAWN

Michelle Barker

Michelle Barker's newest novel My Long List of Impossible Things *came out in 2020 with Annick Press. She is the author of the award-winning novel* The House of One Thousand Eyes *and the historical picture book* A Year of Borrowed Men. *Her fiction, non-fiction, and poetry have appeared in literary reviews around the world. Michelle holds an MFA in creative writing from UBC and works in Vancouver as a senior editor at* The Darling Axe. *Michelle's story 'MVP' won the 2017 SiWC Storyteller's Award and appears in* Pulp Literature *Issue 18, Spring 2018. 'Respawn' was an honourable mention for the same award, now renamed The Jack Whyte Storyteller's Award, in 2021.*

Respawn

Returning to his childhood home always made Mervin feel like he was aging in reverse. "Respawn," his teenage son Jamie would shout whenever they came to visit—which was not often enough according to Mervin's mother, though too often for Mervin's liking. But life was nothing like the video games Mervin and Jamie played together. You didn't get a chance to start over, no matter how much you needed one.

That morning he'd gotten a jump on the weekend traffic out of the city and had arrived at his parents' home before supper. It was mid-spring, and there was still daylight. The lawn was trimmed, the garden weeded, and someone's sprinkler tick-ticked in the distance. Theirs was the nicest home on the street, as his parents liked to remind him. But these days, his dad was getting too old for climbing ladders, and there were eaves to clean out and moss growing on the roof. Why call a professional who knew how to do this stuff properly when you could get your son to drive up five hours and bungle the job? He parked his old VW in front and braced himself for a snarky comment about the car. The Bazou, Jamie called it. It leaked in the rain and smelled like spoiled milk. The check-engine light constantly dared Mervin to blink.

His mother appeared at the door, wearing an apron. "What, no Nancy? No Jamie?" She frowned at the car. The way she favoured her right side meant her hip was bothering her.

"Hello to you, too." Mervin plodded up the cement path with his bag and gave her a hug. The scent of pot roast hung in the air and made his stomach growl. He would have happily brought Jamie, but that would have also meant bringing his wife. Besides, the visits with Nancy were getting awkward. You could hide a failing marriage for the length of one supper, but doing it for a whole weekend was harder.

"I made up your old room for Jamie," his mother said. "But you go ahead and stay there. You can be a teenager again."

Jesus. That was the last thing he wanted to be. He slipped off his scuffed brown shoes and poked his head into the living room where his dad was watching baseball with the volume up, glasses perched low on his nose. His parents were getting older. It startled him to see it. Back in the city, every day was a repeat of the one before, until it felt like time never moved forward—and yet here, time's thumbprints were everywhere.

Mervin took the carpeted stairs up. Even though his mother had aired his old room, there was an underlying musky smell to it that took him back to popping pimples and wearing too much Old Spice. His *Reach for the Top* certificates hung on the wall, and a *Star Wars* quilt covered the bed. "Were you a nerd in high school?" Jamie had asked once. Not all his questions had been so easy to laugh off. Another time, he'd asked what Mervin had wanted to be when he grew up.

Not the manager of a corner grocery store, that was for sure. Who put that in their yearbook, except as a joke? Mervin had dreamed of travelling. He'd imagined himself in a profession they made movies about: archaeology, or something that involved an adventurous hat and pants with lots of pockets. And then Jamie was conceived.

"Supper's ready," his mother called. He rumbled down the stairs, and she made a comment about him still thumping around like an elephant. Nothing had changed.

She set down a glass of milk at the table and said, "So. How's Nancy?" She gave him a pointed look, like she wanted to start something, like the whole visit had nothing to do with eaves and moss and everything to do with *how is your marriage really going* and *can't you do anything right?*

Mervin mumbled, "Fine," and cut into the roast on his plate.

"Saw Frank Ballashine at the gas station the other day," his father said.

Mervin wouldn't look up.

"He's a police officer," his mother said with pride, as if Ballashine was the son she really wanted.

"Good for him," Mervin said. Now he regretted coming alone. If he'd brought Jamie, they could have gone into the living room after dinner and played *Grand Theft Auto* with the volume down. He could have disappeared into the game the way he did at home — except at home he played with the volume high because he knew it drove Nancy crazy. You're not sixteen anymore, she'd shout over the gunfire.

No, he was not. He was nearing forty, losing his hair and working on a second chin — though that didn't stop him from asking his father to pass the gravy. Cutlery clattered against plates in the silent room until his mother said, "Have you considered marriage counselling?"

"Faye," his father said.

"Well, really. Someone needs to speak up."

Mervin stood and took his plate to the kitchen. Then he got his coat.

"Where are you going?" his mother said. "I thought we could visit. I'll make tea."

He needed something stronger than tea.

The sky was fading into darkness as the neon lights at Hooley's flashed up ahead. Hooley's was the place that used to serve Mervin and his friends alcohol when they were underage. Mervin smiled at the memories and pulled into the parking lot. The plan was to sit at the bar, catch his breath, and prepare himself mentally for the rest of the weekend. He parked beside a tow truck with a fancy white Mercedes hitched on the back and couldn't help but chuckle. *Steal a tow truck.* It was one of the *GTA-V* missions. Jamie would have loved it.

He pulled open the bar's heavy wooden door and was assaulted by a rush of beer smell, country music, and laughter. Great. He'd have to sit alone watching sports highlights and chatting up the bartender. This wasn't a good idea. He was turning to leave when someone called, "Mervin?"

Keep walking. Anyone who still knew him in this crappy town was guaranteed to be someone he didn't want to see.

Before he made it to the door, a pair of hands grabbed him by the shoulders, and suddenly a face he would never forget — though God knows he'd tried — was right in front of him. The sharp cheekbones and full lips; the perfect gel-sculpted haircut.

"It *is* you. Holy shit."

Mervin blinked as though there might be a way out of this.

"Edward Thurmon. Don't break my heart and say you don't remember me."

Mervin gave a nervous laugh. "Of course I do."

"We were heading out," Edward said. "But we'll stay for a quick drink." *We* included the tall man behind him wearing skinny jeans and a muscle-hugging T-shirt, whom Edward introduced as David, his date. "You must be here for the reunion," he added, pulling him toward the bar and ordering three vodka tonics.

"Reunion?" Mervin said once they were settled on stools. "You mean high school?"

"What else?" Edward faced him, turning his back on David. Behind him, David pulled out his phone and began texting. "Don't tell me you're not coming."

"I didn't know about it." As if that were the reason Mervin wouldn't go. Twenty years wasn't enough time away from those people. And wouldn't it be grand, rolling up in the Bazou and introducing himself as the manager of Lucky's Market. *Fame or Shame*, another *GTA-V* mission; it could have been the theme of every high school reunion.

"I can't believe how long it's been," Edward said. "Tell me everything."

His wreck of a life? All Edward had to do was walk outside and see the Bazou hanging on by its last spark plug, the panic button permanently engaged, and he would know.

"Nothing to tell," Mervin mumbled, thankful for the drink the bartender placed in front of him. He took a long cool sip and let the vodka put out the fire.

"You got out of this shithole, I hope?"

Mervin took Edward's outstretched arm to mean not just the bar but the whole town. "I escaped, yes."

Edward rested a hand on Mervin's forearm. "And?"

Mervin knew what he was asking. He wanted to pull his arm away, but the weight of Edward's hand sent shockwaves of memory through him. The party. The kiss that everyone had found out about, including, unfortunately, Frank Ballashine. Mervin remembered the way he had denied it, denied Edward— denied everything he'd felt about it. Not that denial had helped. Thanks to Ballashine, the whole town heard about it, and it had been fame and shame in equal measures.

Beside them, a beefy man gave them a long hard look. He had a mug of beer in one hand, and a big ring of keys sat on the bar next to his coaster.

"I got married." Mervin took his arm away to show them a photo of Nancy.

"Kids?" Edward asked.

"A boy." It was the cookie-cutter life you fell back on when you were too scared of the alternative.

Edward didn't seem disappointed, but he also wasn't surprised. A gold watch glistened on his wrist. He was a lawyer out on the coast. David owned a small bakery specializing in gluten-free products.

"They taste better than you'd think," Edward said, and David frowned.

That could have been you. Maybe not the bakery, but something— something with Edward. Instead of his current life, which felt perpetually like he'd put his pants on backwards.

You never ended up where you'd hoped to be. That was why reunions were such a mistake. They were a barometer. Everyone had the same allotment of time. What had he done in those twenty years besides ordering wilted produce for the store and imagining himself as a character in *GTA*? Their audacity—yes, he could use some of that in his life.

David was asking what Mervin did for a living. Maybe to be polite, or maybe because something about Mervin—the frayed jacket cuffs, the middle-age paunch, his need-a-haircut thinning hair—suggested this would shut down all the attention Edward was paying him.

Mervin felt like skewering him with one of the toothpicks at the bar. "I'm in business," he said, which wasn't entirely a lie.

"Come with us," Edward said. "There's a meet and greet tonight. It'll be fun."

Right. Mervin could picture it. *That you, Merv? Don't look a day over forty, haw haw. Whatcha been up to?* He could fake a strong handshake and throw around words like *financing* and *stock options*.

Thank God Nancy hadn't known about the reunion. She would have insisted on coming, and there'd be no false bravado with her around. She was a stickler for the truth; she knew his salary down to the penny and could probably pinpoint to the year and day the last time they'd had sex.

Edward was watching him. "It's your chance to give them all the middle finger, you know. Success is the best revenge."

Sure—when you were successful. When you could pull up in a sweet ride like one of his gaming heroes. If only he had the expensive watch, the dazzling wife, the job so impressively complicated there was no point bothering to explain it.

Edward could stride into the meet and greet with his spine straight and his head high. He'd lived bravely and on his own terms; he'd never worried about what other people thought of him.

David pointed to his watch. "We're going to be late."

"Right." Edward got to his feet. "You coming? It's a whole-weekend thing."

"I don't know. I—"

"At least call me, so we can catch up properly." He typed his number into Mervin's phone and placed a gentle hand on Mervin's cheek before leaving, creating an unexpected tingle on his skin. Mervin shot a worried glance at David, but he was already on his way out. Edward pushed the door open, it whooshed shut, and they were gone.

Alone at the bar, Mervin was struck all over again by the hollow sound of laughter that didn't include him. Though no one was laughing at him, and that was something.

"Another one?" the bartender asked.

"Make it a double," Mervin said.

When the drink arrived, he downed it in a few gulps.

He was onto the next one when a beer mug thunked on the counter next to him. It was the large man with the ring of keys.

"You're not from here."

"Actually, I am." Though Mervin was pleased it didn't show.

"Then maybe you been gone for too long. We don't take to that fancy-pants bullshit around here."

"Listen," Mervin said. "You've got the wrong idea. I'm not—"

He's going to beat you up. The man had been too much of a coward to take on the three of them.

"Tell you what." He fixed Mervin with reddened eyes. "I'm gonna take a piss. When I get back, you'd best be gone."

He tottered off to the bathroom.

Mervin's heart raced. Some ridiculous streak of gallantry was saying, *Do it, take a punch for Edward. You owe him.* He'd been much braver than Mervin—and much surer of who he was. *A real man would stay and fight.*

Who was Mervin fooling? He wasn't that person, and it wouldn't be just one punch.

The guy had left his keys on the bar. Mervin hesitated. He shouldn't. It was reckless … but yes. *Yes.* He took out the key to the Bazou and switched them. *Here. You can have it.*

With the fat man's keys in his hand, he hustled out the door. This was crazy; it was by far the most daring thing he'd ever done in real life. He felt energized—and maybe more than a little drunk.

Show the gentleman what he's won. Probably not the BMW parked carefully in the far corner of the lot where no one would ding it by accident. More likely the dented pickup truck. There was a fob on the ring. When Mervin pressed it, the tow truck with the white Mercedes on the back lit up. He ran towards it.

What are you doing? All the car thefts he'd ever done had been virtual. He'd never stolen so much as a chocolate bar in real life. *Go back in there and tell him you made a mistake.*

The thing was, he hadn't.

He hoisted himself up into the driver's seat, hand shaking as he fit the key into the ignition. A book sat on the passenger seat: *Meathead: The Science of Great Barbecue and Grilling.* That fit. He started the truck and managed to circle the parking lot without hitting anything. He was pulling onto the highway when the fat man appeared in the rear-view mirror, shaking his fist.

"Welcome to my life, meathead." Mervin laughed and drove away as though it were a game. But this was real, and for once he had control.

So. This was what it felt like to be tough. He was used to the Bazou dragging its butt along the road, barely clearing speed bumps. In this truck, he was on top of the world. The cab smelled like sweat and French fries, and there was a black toolbox on the passenger side floor. If he were the fat guy, Nancy would ask him to fix something and he'd know which tool to use and how to do it.

It took a minute before he realized he was driving out of town. He took the first turn off the highway. The thrill of having stolen a vehicle was already wearing off. The fat man would call the police. There'd be an APB out for a tow truck—not exactly inconspicuous—and there he'd be like a fucking idiot, sitting in the cab, waiting to be arrested. *Who steals a tow truck in real life?* No one, that's who. It only happened in *GTA*.

Okay, hold it together. Did he hear sirens? No, he did not. He turned onto a side street and found himself in a rural area where people kept rusted cars on their front lawns. He parked the tow truck and shut it off. *Think.*

The sky had darkened, and the night was alive with crickets. The truck would be equipped with GPS. They'd find him. Besides which, he'd given the fat man his key. All the police had to do was run the plates. Wouldn't Frank Ballashine love seeing Mervin's name pop up on the computer? He should walk away. Run, in fact. But he didn't want to. What he wanted was the white Mercedes he'd been towing. Maybe he would take it to the meet and greet, and let them all eat their fancy gold watches. Problem? Solution. Trade cars, trade lives.

No. No! This was a terrible idea.

Are you kidding? Stealing a tow truck and making off with the Mercedes? It was brilliant. Wouldn't Michael de Santa in *GTA-V* roll up to his high school reunion in a Mercedes? Sure, he would. Mervin just had to unhitch it. The fat guy could have his truck back and keep the Bazou.

The *Meathead* book wouldn't be of any use, but maybe there was a manual in the glove compartment.

It was locked, but soon enough Mervin found the key. A quick look through the truck manual and he was lowering the Mercedes to the ground. He jumped out of the cab and, with the manual in one hand and his cellphone light in the other, he figured out how to release the car.

Sirens whined in the distance as he flipped through the fat man's key ring for the key to the Mercedes, but it wasn't there. In *GTA: San Andreas*, CJ could hotwire a car in three seconds. Mervin had always found that unrealistic.

The sirens were getting louder. If he had to spend time googling how to hotwire a car, he'd end up in jail. Turns out there was something worse than arriving at a reunion in the Bazou.

The Mercedes was unlocked. He checked for a key under the mat—no. In the glove compartment—no.

The sirens were screaming.

When he felt around under the wheel well, his hand closed on a small box. Inside, there was a key. He couldn't believe his luck. This could be a new beginning for him. Maybe after this, he'd even have the courage to leave Nancy.

He climbed into the car, fit the key in the ignition, and turned it. Nothing happened.

His shoulders tensed.

There were usually two reasons for towing a car.

Reason One: you'd parked it somewhere you shouldn't have.

Reason Two: the damn thing was busted.

This was Reason Two.

He jumped out of the car, dropped the keys, and ran.

Flashing lights illuminated the dark country road. He had to find somewhere to hide. He ran into a neighbouring yard and shoved himself through the open window of a rusted Buick. Car tires crunched across the gravel road and stopped. Doors creaked open and slammed shut. A walkie-talkie crackled, and a man spoke into it, saying he'd located the tow truck and the Mercedes, but not the perp.

The perp. Mervin smiled. That was him.

He peeked over the rim of the car door. The fat guy stood with two police officers, a man and a woman, grumbling about *that faggot who made off with my truck.*

Wait. Was that …? In the dark, it was impossible to tell— and twenty years could be cruel. The male police officer looked a little round at the middle. It was satisfying to think of Ballashine letting himself get pouchy, but Mervin hoped it wasn't him. Ballashine would love to arrest him for boosting a tow truck. He could tell everyone about it at the reunion. *Mervin Clark, that loser. I always knew he wouldn't amount to anything.* Ballashine was the reason Mervin's life had been hell. But … was he? Mervin hadn't seen him in twenty years.

Mervin's heart thumped as the police officers made a perfunctory search of the area. They found the tow truck keys and gave them back to the fat guy. He hitched up the Mercedes, swearing about how Mervin better not think he was getting his piece-of-shit car back.

No worries there. He didn't want it.

The fat guy got into the tow truck and drove away. The police left shortly afterwards. Mervin climbed out of the Buick and watched the tail lights of the squad car grow smaller and eventually disappear.

The night was cool. He would be in trouble, he knew that. Considering the fat guy had his tow truck back, it would hopefully just mean a fine for Mervin, but he'd have to go down to the station and maybe even get fingerprinted. Would that be so bad? Maybe there was a part of him that wanted to get caught. His parents would find out. They'd phone Nancy. Everyone would call it a midlife crisis, say he'd lost control, when the truth was he'd taken control for the first time in his life. This was his chance to respawn for real.

His hands shook as he took out his phone. Maybe Edward had only given him his number to be polite. He'd come to the reunion with a date, after all. Right now, he'd be mingling with all the people who'd made fun of him twenty years ago.

Mervin should have been there with him.

Do it. If it really went wrong, he could just say he needed a lawyer. He pressed the name on his list of contacts and waited.

"Edward? It's me."

THE RAVEN SHORT STORY CONTEST

THE 2021 RAVEN SHORT STORY CONTEST

We caw-led and you answered! The 2021 Raven entries brought to our nest a wonderful, wide-ranging collection of stories. Final judge Leo X Robertson had this to say about the winners:

FIRST PLACE: **Laura Kuhlmann** for 'A Jar of Marmalade'. *Beautiful, unique, great sense of place. Much to think about. I like the central theme also——it's one I think about a lot.*

FIRST RUNNER-UP: **Hannah van Didden** for 'Gerald Bantam Says Goodbye'. *Unique concept with a brilliant sense of dark humour. Ramps up in absurdism——a very entertaining read. Makes you think about death in a more lighthearted way. Who couldn't love that?*

SECOND RUNNER-UP: **Cadence Mandybura** for 'Audrey and the Crow'. *This story considers something I think about often, the notion of how societal constructs are what 'disable' people who may well have been specially designed for unique purposes outside our current paradigms. But it also happens to be a great story with a unique central relationship, told lovingly.*

HONOURABLE MENTION: **Kevin Sandefur** for 'Floaters'. *[This story] almost made it into my top three. Beautiful, surreal concept, grippingly told.*

Read on for 'A Jar of Marmalade' and 'Gerald Bantam Says Goodbye'. And look for 'Audrey and the Crow' and 'Floaters' in an upcoming issue.

Congratulations to the other shortlisted authors as well:

Rosie Arcane for 'Pumpkin'
Soramimi Hanarejima for 'Shadow Work'
Alan Sincic for 'Just The Way I Like It'
PG Streeter for 'The Perils of Temporal Ascension'
KT Wagner for 'A Harrowing Beyond the Furrows'
Emile Wood for 'The Plant Thing'

Our thanks to Leo X Robertson for his time and talent, and to all of our submitting authors for sharing their words and supporting *Pulp Literature*.

Laura Kuhlmann is a medical writer and former cancer researcher, currently living in Rockville, Maryland. Her short stories and flash fiction have been published online and in print by Reflex Fiction, Semiahmoo Arts Society, and Carrick Publishing in their anthology A Grave Diagnosis. *In 2020, her short story 'Glimpse of a Goddess' was the runner-up for our Hummingbird Flash Fiction Prize, and it can be found in Issue 29, Winter 2021. Laura is currently editing her first novel—— a mystery that brings together narcotics detectives and scientists in the hunt for novel synthetic drugs.*

Hannah van Didden writes where the story takes her——usually somewhere dark but truthful, often beautiful. You will find pieces of her in places such as Tahoma Literary Review, Crannóg, Southerly, Atticus Review, Southword Journal, *and* Pulp Literature. *Her modern-day fable 'The Lion' appeared in Issue 27, Summer 2020.*

A Jar of Marmalade

BY LAURA KUHLMANN

At first I couldn't see anything wrong with the girl. She seemed to sleep peacefully in the rickety bed, covered by a yellowing sheet that was coming apart at the seams — standard issue for a small hospital in 1970 provincial Romania. The smell of bleach was overpowering. Silvia, the young nurse who had dragged me to the room, was catching her breath beside me. Her face was red and sweaty from the marathon she had run to find me — the only paediatrician on the night shift.

"Doctor Bernevig, your husband called again," the head nurse said from the doorway.

"I'll call him later." I waved her out of the room. "Could you open the window, Silvia?"

She squeezed herself between the table and the girl's bed and fought with the window's locking mechanism. It probably hadn't been opened in weeks. Most of my colleagues were convinced fresh air made illness worse, but I'd seen otherwise.

I leaned over the girl and shook her shoulder.

"Maria? Maria?"

She didn't move.

"I've been trying to wake her up for an hour," Silvia said as she cracked the window open.

The two girls sharing the other bed in the room buried themselves under their blanket. I touched the radiator — it was lukewarm and leaking.

"I thought she was just in deep sleep," Silvia continued. "I figured she could take the antibiotic half an hour later. Since then I've tried cold water, ammonia . . . I even poked her with a needle."

I looked at Maria, a thin twelve-year-old with long brown hair. I had admitted her that morning. Recurrent urinary infections after strep throat. The doctor in her village had diagnosed her with nasal polyps and recommended her to an ear, nose, and throat specialist in the city. Maria's family had taken out their horse and wagon and brought her to Buzău for a polyp removal surgery. I suspected the recurrent urinary infections had been caused by the last course of antibiotics. So I started her on a different antibiotic while I waited for the antibiogram results from the lab. I don't like waiting. Waiting kills. I knew that all too well.

Maria's hand was warm and clammy, but she didn't have a fever. Her pulse was strong, her pupils equal and reactive. Why couldn't we wake her up?

I glanced at the table. Maria's family had left a small jar of marmalade for her. That jar was empty now.

"Did she finish that today?" I asked Silvia.

"Yes. Her father says she always had a sweet tooth." Silvia's lower lip trembled. "Maybe I shouldn't have let her finish it?"

I shook my head. "And then she would have eaten what? God

knows we don't have anything resembling food in this hospital."

Yet Maria's appetite for sweets bothered me. It could worsen her urinary infection. Or …

I lowered my head and opened her mouth. Her breath smelled like acetone.

"What's wrong?" Silvia asked.

"Had she had anything else to eat?"

"I don't know, it was a busy day."

Acetone breath could mean one of two things: too much sugar in her blood, or too little. Why such opposite conditions would lead to the same symptom wasn't clear to me. But that didn't matter right now.

Maria was in a coma. Was it a diabetic coma? Or one brought on by low blood sugar? If it was the former, she needed insulin. But if it was the latter, insulin would cause her blood sugar to plummet further and kill her.

Our lab opened at seven in the morning. By then it would be too late.

I explained my reasoning to Silvia. She listened and nodded, her thin lips tightly pressed together. I could think of only one way to determine what was causing Maria's coma.

"I'll need to taste her urine," I told Silvia.

If Maria had diabetes, her urine would be sweet.

"I'll install a probe," Silvia said.

The thought of tasting my patient's urine made me queasy.

"I'll go rinse my mouth," I told Silvia.

In the bathroom I passed cold water over my face and neck and up my arms, and then I swallowed a handful. The water in Buzău tasted as fresh as the water in my parents' well. It brought back memories of two summers ago, when we took Eliza to the cottage … My throat closed. Not now. I needed to focus.

I put on my glasses and passed a hand over my sagging cheeks. I pulled away from my reflection and returned to the nurses' room.

The old head nurse was boiling a pot full of glass syringes and needles on the stove. She fished a gauze out of the bubbling cauldron. Syringe needles were pinned in the gauze and she plucked them out, then placed them on the disinfected metal tray to dry.

I grabbed a syringe, needle, and insulin. Maria most likely had diabetes. It would explain both her cravings and her urinary infection. Of course, I still needed to taste her urine to be sure.

I walked back to the room. Silvia was rinsing her mouth at the sink in the corner of the room.

"You don't need to taste it, Doctor. It's syrup."

My vision clouded. Again, I had arrived too late. I gripped Silvia's shoulder and thanked her in a shaky voice. She smiled.

We administered the insulin at 1:30 am. Maria woke up an hour later.

The carriage narrowly missed me as I crossed the road to my house. The old driver steered the horse away and yelled at me to watch where I was going. While I disliked piles of horse manure littering the streets, I also knew that most of my patients weren't able to reach me without a carriage. Half-asleep, I pushed the gate open while taking in deep breaths of the cold morning air. I tiptoed inside the house, hoping the thick carpet would muffle my steps. The warm hallway smelled like incense. Last night's emergency had wiped from my mind the memory of the priest, only an hour before I had left for my shift, swinging his censer up and down and singing 'Eternal Remembrance' in a deep baritone. Eliza had always loved the spicy scent. Could she smell it wherever she was now?

I knew I wouldn't be able to sleep. So I headed for the front room, where I sometimes saw patients, hoping David would sleep for a couple more hours.

"When are you going to remember that *I* need you too?"

I jumped and turned. My husband was watching me from the threshold of our bedroom. The bags under his eyes told me his had also been a sleepless night.

"We had an emergency."

"You couldn't at least call me back? I used all my connections in the Party to get a phone installed, and you only use it to talk to your patients."

"David, I can't just ignore them at the end of my shift."

Why couldn't I tell him how much I appreciated his effort to get us a phone? Some people waited years to be allowed one. And people like us, people who inherited a home, were least likely to get approved. I still didn't understand why the Party had allowed David to keep the house. Maybe it was because I came from poverty, thus alleviating his sin of being born to a well-to-do middle-class family. Maybe it was because I often rushed in the middle of the night to treat the son of the local Party secretary.

David stepped away from the door, leaving room for me to pass. "Come to bed."

"I'm not tired. Maybe I'll read something first."

"Stop reading her chart. Please." He looked at me. "It wouldn't have mattered if they had given her antibiotics earlier or not."

"That's not true, and you know it," I hissed.

"We can't bring Eliza back. Come to bed."

There was no point. What he wanted, I couldn't give.

I didn't answer. Didn't move. He sighed and closed the door. The silence that followed told me he was still waiting, close to the door, hoping I'd heed his quiet call.

Instead I walked to the end of the hallway, to our daughter's bedroom. David had allowed me to keep it as it had been a year ago, the bed freshly made, the desk stacked with Eliza's notebooks. Her school photo hung on the wall. In it, Eliza wore the standard-issue uniform, the chequered white-and-blue shirt with a dark-blue apron. Her hair was short. I hadn't allowed her to grow it. We had constant fights about that. To atone for my decision, I had allowed her to wear those ridiculous pompoms on her hairband, two cheap white flowers that looked like crumbling ears. Eliza stared at the camera, her thin lips frozen in an uncomfortable smile. Her hand gripped a pen at an odd angle. My daughter was left-handed. The teachers forced her to write with her right. Oh, the cries until she agreed to play their game in the classroom. At home she always wrote with her left.

My beautiful, stubborn daughter.

I lay down on top of the yellow comforter, buried my face in her pillow. It smelled of fresh laundry, all scent of her removed.

The smell of vomit was also removed. Her last hours in this room had been a hot torture. I should have pressed the doctor to admit us to the hospital sooner. Should have fed her antibiotics myself, when I suspected meningitis, and not waited for a confirmation.

This won't happen to another parent, I promised myself. Antibiotics first, as soon as I suspect a bacterial infection.

Treating the son of a Party secretary had its perks. Party

members can travel abroad. I could ask for medicine not available in Romania. I stashed the expensive drugs in my daughter's room for those patients *I* thought needed it. The Party couldn't control who received it. This time I was in control.

David wanted to redecorate the room, plan for a new child. I hadn't told him we had missed that window, that my body would no longer cooperate with our desires to have another baby.

I fell asleep on top of Eliza's bed, unsure about the honesty I owed my husband.

Saturday afternoon the cemetery was empty. Most people were still at work. I roamed the paths to my daughter's grave, carrying red and white carnations—her favourite. I laid my bouquet next to the one of roses already waiting at the bottom of her cross. I took off my glove and caressed the roses' frozen petals. David must have brought them in the morning before he left for work.

Guilt crept up on me again. When would I tell David we couldn't have another child? My chest tightened every time I tried to say the words out loud. It was as if postponing their release could offset my menopause. I walked home, aware that I could no longer delay my confession.

A carriage was stopped in front of our gate. The pungent smell of dung and hay reached me from across the street. Maria and her father were pacing in front of my fence.

"Maria," I called.

She turned and waved at me. Her jaw was tense, her throat probably still sore from the polyp-removal surgery.

"Doctor Bernevig," Maria's father said. He took off his hat and started turning it in his hands. "We wanted to thank you for what you've done for us."

"Please, don't mention it."

I suspected they wanted to give me a present, as was customary at our hospital. I could tell they were too poor to afford the coffee or cigarettes some of my colleagues demanded. Instead I heard a rooster thrashing inside their carriage.

"Please, you owe me nothing," I said in an alarmed voice.

Maria's father took out the rooster and a long knife, ready to chop the bird's head right there, in front of my courtyard. After a long negotiation he agreed to let the poor beast live and take it back home with them.

"At least have some eggs," Maria's father said.

I sighed and accepted a small bag filled with eggs carefully wrapped in old newspaper.

"And this." He handed me a jar of marmalade. "Since my daughter can't have it anymore."

He had brought a bag full of jars.

"Maria will have to be very careful with her diet," I said as I opened the gate and let them in. "But she can keep her blood sugar under control with a little care and the insulin I prescribed."

I led them to my front room and invited them to sit in front of the woodstove as I rekindled the fire.

"Maria, I want to make sure you know how to administer the insulin to yourself," I said after I washed my hands.

Maria's father wrung his hands as he backed out of the room. "Yes, yes, she wanted to ask you about ... about ... I'll wait outside."

We remained quiet while he stepped out. Through the room's window, we saw him rest under the linden tree in my yard. I looked at Maria, waiting to hear what had really prompted the visit.

Maria's cheeks grew pink.

"What is it?"

She had gotten her first period in the hospital. Silvia had tried to explain to her what it meant. I hadn't known that Maria's mother had died years ago. Maria had no one to answer her questions.

I walked to my wardrobe and retrieved the silky cotton package I kept for myself. Hard to find something of this quality in a local pharmacy. I wouldn't be needing it anymore. I taught Maria how to improvise a cotton pad for her period. It was better than using a cloth as she had planned. She watched me carefully, her cheeks still red.

"There's nothing to be ashamed of." My voice was firm, which made her blush even more. "It's natural. You're a woman now."

The clock echoed in the quiet hallway after their departure. I had planned a similar talk with my daughter. Today, that plan had served me well.

I picked up the bags Maria's father had brought, walked to the kitchen, and arranged the jars of marmalade at the back of our storage cupboard. I kept one jar out and peeled away the sealing cellophane. The sweet smell tickled my nostrils—rose flowers. David would love it.

Tonight, I needed to thank David for giving me free rein over both Eliza's room and the front room—two rooms where I could tend my children and watch them grow.

I cut a slice of bread and spread the scented rose marmalade on top. The saltiness of my tears mixed in with the overpowering sweetness of the rose petals. I took another bite, before cutting another slice of bread.

GERALD BANTAM SAYS GOODBYE

BY HANNAH VAN DIDDEN

After fifty-seven years of not following the crowd, Gerald Bantam succumbed. Mrs Amanda Ericsson pushed him to it in the end. They ran into each other in the cheese section of the local deli and took their conversation to the counter.

"You know, Gerald," she said, peering over those purple-rimmed spectacles that otherwise hung from the clear plastic chain under her jowl, "you don't have to say no just to be different."

"She has the point." Evan, the deli owner, grinned at them from behind the service counter, his dark hair caught up in a slick that appeared to have leaked into his navy apron. He scanned Gerald's paper-covered selections, and thin fingers flourished around the payment amount on the LCD display. "It gives you more of the good life with a loved one. You loved your wife, yes?"

Gerald gathered up his edam and mortadella, and nodded an emphatic goodbye.

Behind his polite smile, he was tired. He was exhausted by his neighbours' relentless demonstrations of cheer — at the shops,

walking their critters, rolling their front lawns into submission —
in the constant company of their loved ones. He was lonely. Della
had been their social planner and, with her passing, the kids' visits
had slowed. But Daniel, Molly, Molly's unspeaking beau, and Kara
all came home for Christmas.

They made not a sound as they processed the sight of their
dead mother on her favourite chair.

Then Molly jangled a bejewelled arm around her father's
shoulders. "Look at you, keeping up with modern trends."

"I didn't think you were going to," said Daniel.

Kara, who was the youngest and most like him, shook her
head. "How could you?" she whispered.

"It was what your mother wanted," Gerald replied.

"I like," Molly said. "This way we'll always have her with
us, right?"

That was when Kara ran sobbing into her old room, which,
as she was about to discover, had been refurbished as a shrine
for her late mother.

When a man in Texas killed and stuffed his parents, the incident
invoked a worldwide debate and a temporary ban on all stuffings.

Taxidermists were up in arms, as were those who recognized
people-stuffing as an emerging market. They wrote letters, pick-
eted houses of parliament, commissioned thought pieces. And
psychologists wrote papers about the many issues that could be
postponed or resolved by allowing an alive person to keep their
loved one within the family unit after death. Children could air
grievances without the parent answering back — or they could
find catharsis in enacting something like murder, except that it
wasn't murder because you can't re-kill a person — and a parent

need never feel the loss of a child because they would always have them there, preserved.

Lawmakers and ethicists cited composting bags and the circle of life in conceding that a non-living once-living thing was indeed dead and gone, and redefined a live thing as 'alive'; dead things could be stuffed so long as the alive person(s) benefiting from the stuffing did not cause the once-living thing to die.

Gerald had watched all of this unfold and refold on the evening news, with Della by his side, the year before she died.

"That's one thing I never want to see here," Gerald had scoffed.

"Don't be so quick to judge, Gerry," Della said. "Just imagine it. Keeping our family together — maybe even our community."

"It's crazy."

"I'd have you stuffed."

"You would not. I forbid it."

"When you're dead, I can do what I like with you. If I want you stuffed, you'll be stuffed."

"You would really do that?"

She had smiled in her wicked, teasing way, and he'd sulked for hours after, even though no such practice had reached their neighbourhood. Not at that time. It was months before their street got its first stuffee — or 'stuffy', as they came to be known.

Mrs Amanda Ericsson, who'd had her dog, Boska, taxidermied years beforehand, decided to stuff her mother-in-law in a pose and dress appropriate for a perpetual tea party. The pained look on her mother-in-law's face did not bother her one jot.

"Ethel is as those who loved her knew her," Mrs Amanda Ericsson said.

Everyone in the street commented that, since the stuffing, Mrs Amanda Ericsson did seem to have an extra zing about the way she moved, and that maybe this stuffing thing wasn't such a bad idea. Unquestionably crazy, but good crazy.

"It's lovely you've all been so accepting of Ethel," Mrs Amanda Ericsson said at the neighbourhood barbeque she hosted to re-welcome her mother-in-law. "What a shame stuffing wasn't around when my Terence died."

She cast her eyes towards some faraway place beyond the back fence.

"Why don't you stuff him next?" suggested Mr Anthony Farrowsmith-Crowley, who lived two doors down.

"Would that be decent?" Mrs Amanda Ericsson held a hand to the glasses that dangled at her chest. "Terence has been buried two years now."

"The smell!" Mr Anthony Farrowsmith-Crowley's daughter, Chandra, who was also standing by, lapped at the icy liquid around the rosemary in her glass. She was a sommelier-in-training but drank spirits at parties because she didn't want to mix business with pleasure.

"He'd have been fully embalmed." Mr Anthony Farrowsmith-Crowley looked down his nose at his daughter. "And buried in a thick wooden casket. If I were you, I'd give it a go. In fact," he said, slamming his ale onto the thick wood of the outside table, "why don't we head down there and dig him up?"

"Really? You would all come with me to do that?" Mrs Amanda Ericsson gulped her Chardonnay. She hadn't visited her husband's grave since his burial, on account of her fear of cemeteries and the accompanying potential for possession by vengeful spirits.

"Why not?"

"I guess we could use Terence's tools. I haven't touched them since. And he did have an excellent array of shovels."

"It's settled, then. We'll all pitch in." Her neighbour puffed up his chest and turned to address the other guests. "We are going to save Terence. Anyone who's interested in a good old-fashioned grave digging, follow me!"

The call to action sparked a unified cheer and a stampede that moved in a crow's line to the shed before trampling the back fence, the herd of heels and boots and patterned brogues cracking plant pots, piercing blow-up ornaments, and divotting the lawn on their way.

Only Gerald and Della remained behind. In those strange moments, they pondered what had happened, finished their drinks, and walked home.

Della returned to her neighbour the next day with a handcrafted 'Welcome back, Terence' card, made with the quilling skills she had picked up one crafternoon at the library. However, Terence, she was informed, would not be home for another week.

When he did reappear, he did look more prune-faced than his image in old photos, but this was how they all remembered him anyway.

Terence's stuffing and his wife's subsequent elation triggered a spate of stuffings on their street. It became the norm when someone passed on. And instead of a funeral, the new stuffy would be guest of honour at their own welcome-back barbeque — or 'welbie', as they came to be known.

When Della passed on, Gerald knew what was expected.

Because Della loved to read, she had been stuffed with her hands open. He meant to change the book every week. This week's book was the same she'd held since the start — *Anne of Green Gables*, which she'd read to a seven-year-old Kara. That might have been why Kara had run off as she did. Or maybe it was the fact he had already let her grieve.

In the days to come, he and Molly took turns trying to talk Kara out of her old room, but she refused to move. Still, so long as she was out before the new year was in, she wouldn't miss her mother's welbie.

Not long after the ban on stuffing was revoked, stuffies began to take over the public and private spaces of the world. The evening news was crammed with tales of how alive people could hardly move for all the dead ones: stuffies filled houses, malls, beaches, parks, roads. The legal system overflowed with people suing other people for destruction of their stuffies, or stuffies inadvertently causing injury or death by virtue of their place-ment, thereby creating more stuffies. Hospitals, stuffers, and law enforcers could not keep up.

People started to take the law into their own hands, and families of accused stuffy-destroyers were themselves stuffed in the night. The vigilante, or vigilantes, responsible became known as the Night Stuffer—and BC Comics would immortalize the Night Stuffer by creating an entire comic book series about him, her, or them (even in the comic it was unclear).

But in Gerald's neighbourhood, stuffies and alive people appeared to coexist in harmony.

Mr Anthony Farrowsmith-Crowley was the first guest to arrive at Della's welbie, accompanied by his alive mistress and dead wife.

"I'd never have dreamt of putting them in the same room while Sandy was alive. But look at them now." His dead wife was smiling; his girlfriend was not. With an inward lean, he asked, "Who did Della's stuffing?"

"Malcolm Paisley of Paisley Stuffings and Upholstery," said Gerald, and his neighbour nodded and hmm-ed in a way that made Gerald think he must have gone to the right place.

Mrs Amanda Ericsson was next in. Terence was propped upright on a trolley with Boska the dog and Ethel on either side, and he was not holding up well. His left ear sagged into his cheek. A sign of poor craftsmanship, perhaps? Gerald hoped that Terence had not been stuffed by Malcolm Paisley of Paisley Stuffings and Upholstery.

"How delightful to see you, Gerald!" she cried. "And Della's looking well."

Mrs Amanda Ericsson had never thought Gerald was delightful to see when Della was alive. He could not recall having ever been interesting to his neighbours during Della's lifetime, yet a whole street's worth of them — past and present — were now overtaking his back lawn.

Della sat at the head of the outdoor setting, holding a tray of smoked salmon hors d'oeuvres in place of *Anne of Green Gables* and watching over a Black Forest cake rimmed with gold candles. She wore magenta lipstick and tortoiseshell sunglasses, courtesy of Molly's styling.

Molly was on drinks, her unspeaking beau offering finger food. Mr Anthony Farrowsmith-Crowley led a one-way argument with his former missus, his back to the girlfriend, who had not been properly introduced to anyone. She laughed effusively at something Daniel said and unplugged her heels from the lawn to move closer. And, as Daniel ignored Molly's call for "little help, please!" from the drinks table, he side-eyed Evan the deli owner, who appeared to be making himself comfortable with Chandra: she arrived late but brought vodka for the non-existent punch. Mrs Amanda Ericsson kept to her own contingent of stuffed guests.

When Kara ventured out of her old room, it was to brood in the seat next to her mother.

Gerald recognized others in the swarm of faces, most of whom had been dead for some time. The stuffed guests, who outnumbered the living by two to one, were propped up against plants and furniture. They became tripping hazards as the welbie progressed.

Ethel was the first to suffer an injury, an arm broken clean off by another guest's backwards stumble.

Mrs Amanda Ericsson pointed a bony finger, and the party fell silent. "You did that on purpose," she said.

"I really didn't," said a girl who had been so still and soundless that, up to that point, Gerald had assumed she was a stuffy.

The older woman lashed out with a screech, her open palm missing the girl, who had ducked. The mother of Evan the deli owner bore the brunt of the attack.

In rising to his feet, Evan knocked into the late Mrs Anthony Farrowsmith-Crowley, who amazed everyone with the distance she was able to cover unassisted. She toppled Terence when she touched down, to gasps from the crowd.

Then it was on.

Food, cutlery, glasses, and plates flew over the yard, followed by shoes, limbs, skin, and stuffing.

When the knife hit Della, the melee stopped. All eyes turned to Gerald.

Della's head had been cleaved from cheek to neck. Skin curled from the gash, spilling polyester filler over the smoked salmon hors d'oeuvres; one side of her cake had been crushed by a stray hand. Kara remained in the seat next to her mother, her eyes filling with tears. No one uttered a word. Della's damage may have been minor in comparison to the destruction that had befallen other stuffies, but it had horrified the party into stillness.

Gerald opened his mouth to lecture, but he saw how they were. Many were holding their heads in their hands, and most were sporting minor injuries. Some had begun to sob and moan.

"Go home. All of you," he said, and they hobbled off, guarding their wounds as they retrieved their dead.

Gerald piled up the mess left behind and lit a bonfire in the back corner of the yard. He buried his stuffed wife under the lemon tree with his children looking on. And Daniel, Molly, Molly's unspeaking beau, and Kara stayed on at the house with him to eat the good half of the cake and remember Della as she was.

COMIC COLLECTION

Hurricane Nancy

Nancy's work goes back to the East Village Other, *circa 1966. Trailblazer Trina Robbins names Nancy as an inspiration to move forward with her Wimmen's Comix movement. In fact, Nancy was a founding member of Robbins's all-women comic book series, It Ain't Me, Babe, which began in 1970. Sixty-five pieces of Nancy's cartoon art are in The Billy Ireland Cartoon Library and Museum at Ohio State University. Nancy currently produces cartoons influenced by the oddities of current life and more.*

Turtle

Everyone's Got an Opinion

Mandala for Handling Stress

We Can Work It Out

Mandala for Cheerfulness

Create Despite All Odds

THE SHEPHERDESS: ARTIFICE

JM Landels

On her ascent through the social circles of seventeenth-century France — from shepherdess, to maid, to physician's apprentice, to lady-in-waiting — a dangerous object has fallen into Toinette's hands: a letter opener housing a hidden stiletto with a poisoned blade. Having discerned its maker, she now needs to know whom it was designed to kill.

JM Landels *is torn between travelling the world to teach writing and swordfighting, and never leaving her idyllic farm in Langley, BC. Her debut series, fantasy bestseller* Allaigna's Song: Overture, *and the sequels,* Aria *and* Chorale, *are available from Pulp Literature Press and Amazon. You can follow her adventures with pen and sword at jmlandels.stiffbunnies.com.*

$\mathcal{T}$HE SHEPHERDESS: ARTIFICE

It was strange to be back in Paris again, away from the bizarrely formed intrigue of Versailles. Dressing as a boy made sitting Marteau's trot more convenient but no less comfortable, and I wished for Madame's carriage, no matter how stuffy and stiffly sprung the ride in the other direction had been. Henri and I had set out at dawn, he on a livery mare I insisted he hire to spare Marteau his great weight. I wished now that I had taken the mare instead, as she clearly had an amble far easier to ride.

We didn't go to the house—it would take too long to wake it up from its cold and shuttered state. Instead we took two rooms on rue St Antoine. The following morning over bread and warm wine—how I missed Ahmed's Turkish coffee already—I informed Henri that he would accompany me to the Ile de la Cité.

This morning I was dressed as a girl once again, which seemed to give the innkeeper no pause. I left Henri holding the horses on the main thoroughfare. The workshop entrance was on a tiny ruelle west of Nôtre Dame. The sign on the door simply read 'Van Nuyens'.

I knocked. A dog yipped from inside. I waited, knocked again, and tried the handle.

"M'sieur Van Noyen?" I called, sticking my head through the door.

"Van Nuyens," a voice corrected me irritably, before mumbling "damned French" as a small white dog galloped to the door, yapping frenetically. Its owner appeared from the same back room. His hair was shorn as if for a wig, but it was not shorn recently or well. Whitish tufts stuck out in all directions, like a half-blown dandelion. The dog and he were much of a pair.

"I am closed," he said in heavily accented French. "No commissions till the new year. At least." He grabbed the dog by the scruff of its neck to prevent it from leaving and pushed the door with his other hand.

I put my sabot in the way. "No commission, m'sieur."

"Then I certainly don't want to see you." He gave the door a little slam, which made a satisfying clack against the sabot.

"Just a question, m'sieur." I jingled the small purse I held. "It won't take a minute of your time."

A calloused hand shot out. I placed a single pistole in the dirt-seamed palm.

"Ask, then."

"Not in the street, m'sieur."

"*Pest,*" he muttered, opening the door. I stepped into the room.

He picked up the dog, which emitted a continuous high-pitched growl. "A minute," the man said. "Or less." He glanced at the soot-streaked hearth, above which sat a fine brass clock, incongruously shiny in the dingy accommodation.

I placed the purse on the weathered table in the centre of the room and pulled the Duchess's monocle from my pocket.

"Did you make this, m'sieur?" I asked, holding it out for him to examine.

He barely glanced at it. "Yes, what's wrong with it? I have no time for repairs either."

"Nothing. It works beautifully," I said, slipping it back into my pocket. I reached down the front of my bodice next. "But I think it means you made this as well."

I withdrew the letter opener and placed it on the table, nearer me than him, without taking my gaze from his face.

His eyes were set deep below grizzled brows, making his expression hard to read in the yellow light of the horn window, but he blinked before replying. "No."

"Look more closely," I said, and reached down to pick it up.

More quickly than I had thought an old man could, he lunged for it. But my hand was closer, and he was holding a dog.

I snatched it away, stepped back, and sprang the catch, releasing the stiletto. He froze, his face inches from the needle of the blade I held. Was it fear of the weapon only, or did he fear poison as well?

"For whom did you make this, M'sieur Nuyens?"

"If I tell you that, it will be the death of both of us." He backed away slowly, angling towards his back room. I followed, trying not to let him see my hand tremble.

"If you do not, it will be the death of you anyway."

He definitely feared poison—I could see it in the way he watched the blade. If not for that fear he could have simply overpowered me, for though he was old, I was slight. But just to be sure, I added, "There is a very large man, with a dog five times the size of yours, waiting for me. He has pistols and a sword. I suggest, sir, you tell me what you know."

Van Nuyens's retreating foot crossed the threshold into his back room, and the old man ducked, scuttled backward, and slammed the connecting door in my face.

It struck the outstretched blade in my hand so hard I feared the needle-like metal would snap. Instead it stuck. The door rebounded open and snatched the weapon from my hand.

As I struggled to pull it from the wood, I looked up in time to see Van Nuyens dive over a workbench strewn with tools and throw open a cupboard. At last, I wrenched free the poignard, and only then did it occur to me to bellow "Henri!" over the frantic yapping of the dog.

Next came a resonant crack, and the wood of the door frame beside my head shattered, sending splinters into my face. I ducked in reflex—too late, if the ball now lodged in the frame had been on target.

"Not another word, mademoiselle," said Nuyens, "or the next goes in your belly."

I straightened and saw the threat in his hand: a stonebow, no bigger than a dinner plate, was levelled at me, the shiny brass ball in its cradle glinting in the light from the forge. Another, twin to the first, dangled spent from his left hand. "Drop the knife," he said.

I let the weapon slide from my fingers. "M'sieur," I said as gently as I could, "my only desire is for answers. Would you risk having to drag my corpse to the Seine over that?"

"I will defend myself from a poissoneuse." He motioned with the stonebow, indicating I should retreat, while he made his way around the workbench. The dog darted forward to harry my feet.

I stepped back, wondering if the wood of the door was proof against the ball, but decided not to trust it entirely. As I pulled the door shut in front of me, I threw myself to the ground. There was another splintering of wood and the ball whistled above me, shattering the horn window opposite. I threw both feet against the door, kicking it back open, hoping to hit Nuyens with it. It would take two hands to reload the bow, and I counted on him being busy with that.

I had no luck on either count. The door banged against the wall, Nuyens well clear of it. The dog dashed though, growling and barking, and I snatched at its collar, holding the noisome creature away from my face. Nuyens had dropped the bow and instead held the letter opener with his sleeve pulled over his hand, as if afraid to touch it. He was not afraid to use it, however.

He was old but wiry. And fast. Like a crow striking a snake, he snatched me by the ankle, and hoisted my foot high in the air, holding the point of the needle blade inches from my stockinged calf.

"Do not move, damsel, or you shall feel the bite of your own venom."

Unlike he, I knew the blade was no longer poisoned. I let fly with my other foot, hitting him in the knee with my heavy wooden clog.

I felt the sting of the blade in my calf as he tumbled on top of me, knocking the air from both of us. He was in more pain than I thought, and I wriggled from beneath him, letting go the dog and rolling to where the weapon lay on the floor once more. The dog, distracted by his master's face so near to him, began wagging and licking as frenetically as he had barked.

"You idiot." I seized the poignard and waved it at Van Nuyens. "This could have been so much less painful."

At that moment, Henri burst into the front room.

"Where have you been?" I groaned as I stood and reordered my skirts.

He looked offended. "I had to tether the horses."

There came an odd sound from the floor where Van Nuyens lay cradling his knee. There were tears streaming down his lined face as he moaned something in Flemish. The dog barked half-heartedly at Henri but continued to try and sop his master's tears.

Henri looked at him, and the disarray of his workshop. "You have a strange notion of talking, mam'selle. Why is this man crying?"

"Forgive me," Nuyens pleaded, clasping his hands. "I am ruined and dead, and now I have taken a young woman to the grave with me."

I grimaced. "This is not a confessional."

"Not to worry, mam'selle. The man's Protestant, I'll warrant." To Nuyens, Henri said, "If you'd kindly answer the lady's questions, we'll be on our way …" His words trailed off as he picked up the sheath of the letter opener.

I stumped over to him and snatched it from his hand.

"Toinette," he said, in what sounded like genuine alarm, "is that blood yours?"

I glanced over my shoulder and saw bright red heel prints from my left sabot upon the worn but immaculately swept floor. I drew up the back of my skirt, unheeding of the two men watching. There was a thin rivulet of blood that stained the greenish-white silk of my hose, running from calf to heel. I cursed myself for wearing my best stockings. What on earth had I been thinking?

The wound wasn't deep—perhaps the stockings had been a good idea after all, for men had been known to be saved from musket balls and bodkins by the grace of a silk undershirt. But the needle-like bodkin had pricked a vein, silk or no. I indelicately placed my foot upon one of Nuyens's work stools and stood like a man, my thumb pressed to the back of my calf.

"What?" I demanded of the blubbering artisan, who still rocked back and forth on the floor. Surely I hadn't broken his knee with that kick. And if he was worried about the mess on his floor, well, he was the one who'd spilled my blood.

He started a reply in Flemish before switching to his accented French. "I have killed you, mademoiselle, as sure as you have killed me."

I stared at him for a moment before replying. "The bodkin is no longer poisoned," I said as if explaining to my sister for the dozenth time how to toss a sheep. "Though clearly you knew it once was. So, Monsieur Van Nuyens, I am unlikely to die from *this* prick. But tell me why I have killed you."

"I have been assured, mam'zelle, that if anyone should trace that weapon back to me, my life would be at an end."

I could not resist a dry jab. "Would it not have been prudent to design it less distinctly, then?"

He looked momentarily offended. "As if my craftsmanship could be mistaken for another's, maker's mark or no." But his shoulders sagged. "I would have made it as plain and crude as a knife from the smithy if I had known that before the work was complete." He looked up at me, his deep-set eyes pleading. "If you have a drop of goodness in your heart, mam'zelle, allow me to leave. Or kill me quickly and do not leave me for the inquisitors."

Henri spoke up. "As a Protestant, I don't doubt that will be the guise of the revenge he receives, mademoiselle. Whatever the truth of his crimes, it would be kinder to kill him."

I gave Henri a black look.

To Nuyens, I said, "Henri will escort you as far as Liège." Henri's head shot up. "He makes a fair bodyguard and he knows the back roads of the country." That was a guess on my part, but Henri didn't protest this piece of information. "In exchange, you will tell us the history of this blade, who bought it, and who the victim was to be."

I had to travel back to Versailles alone. I reluctantly gave Henri the use of Marteau. It was the least I could do, he insisted, after I had volunteered him as Van Nuyens's escort. Or I could come with him to Liège. There seemed to be a sort of hopeful question in his voice. But I hadn't forgiven him for the subterfuge that had put me in Sauvegarde's path, so a loan—a loan only, mind you—of my half of Marteau was all that was needed to settle our books. He would return, I was sure, for Madame was his queen and he the worker bee drawn inexorably back to her. As was I, it seemed.

The coach ride to Versailles was worse than the carriage one way or the horse the other had been. Dressed once more as a boy, I found myself riding on the roof amid the baggage, clinging for dear life as the vehicle swayed and bounced. Better that, though, than crammed between fat old men and fishwives smelling of tobacco, sausage, farts, and unwashed armpits. A sheepfold that hadn't been mucked all year smelled better than that.

The familiar smell of the palais was no better, just different, with its cloying mix of perfumes. I closed the door to Madame's apartments with relief, and with the epiphany that it felt like coming home.

Madame was reading by the fire. She looked up with a smile that welcomed me even more, but her words went straight to the point. "And what did you find, Toinette?"

"The Chevalier de Lorraine," I said.

I removed the letter opener from the stays I wore under my boy's shirt. Madame raised her eyebrows expectantly but, for all that, looked unsurprised.

"The Chevalier gave this as a gift to Monsieur's first wife, Henriette. Of England," I continued.

That did surprise her.

Madame took it from me, turning it over a few times before springing the catch. "To say there was no love lost between Minette and the Chevalier would be the world's greatest understatement," she said as she slid the delicate blade from its disguise. "And it was definitely poisoned, you say?"

"Dr Ahmed confirmed it. And," I pre-empted her next question, "there is no doubt the artisan knew it. It was not created as an innocent tool."

"Did this Van Nuyens put the poison on it himself?"

"He says not. But does that matter? His patron, the Chevalier, commissioned it for such."

She nodded. "So why would the Chevalier give such a gift to Minette?"

"How did she die, Madame?" I asked.

"Not by poison, though many suspected it. She perished from an infection of the stomach."

I picked up the letter opener and examined the long thin needle of the blade. "Henri told me," I observed, "that duellists sometimes survive a fight only to die days or weeks later from poisoning of the blood. A small wound, hardly noticeable, that heals on the outside but festers within." My voice slowed as my mind clicked like the workings of Van Nuyens's clock. I was thinking of sheep who mysteriously die of lockjaw with no injuries upon them. Only later does one discover a tiny puncture wound upon the pastern after their final shearing. "A prick from such a small blade would leave hardly a wound, and might not even be felt beneath the daily pinch of stays." I paused. "Why did Henri go to such pains to take it from Sauvegarde?"

Madame looked at me levelly. "I tell you this with hesitation, Toinette, for it is weighty and dangerous knowledge. Yet I feel you have earned it, and, if used wisely, it could someday save you."

I felt a reluctant chill, like setting my feet in the cold water of a river.

She sat back in her chair, tapping her closed fan against her wrist as she weighed her words. "His Majesty gave it to me."

So startled was I that I dropped the item in question. It spun on the lacquered table like a compass gone mad. Madame picked it up, sheathed it in its innocuous disguise once more, and placed it back on the table.

"I was tasked with disposing of it. Not in a midden, or even in the Seine. I was en route from Versailles to Paris where a smith I trusted would have smelted it. My carriage was waylaid, and my jewels—including the ruby necklace His Majesty had given me—were stolen. Along with this."

I knew without asking. "Sauvegarde." No doubt, the man was causing trouble long before he became a thorn in my side.

She nodded. "It would have been wiser, then, to turn around and tell the King. But Sauvegarde and I have a history. I sent Henri after him, and worked my own connections to try and find out whom he was working for and why they wanted what the King wanted destroyed."

That explained why Henri had come to my aid not once, but twice on my journey from St Geneviève to Paris. "And did you?"

She shook her head. "Not till now. The why obscured the whom.

"So imagine this," she said. "An instrument of assassination. The King wants it gone. The Chevalier de Lorraine wants it back. Why? The Chevalier wants to destroy it himself. He will not trust his lackey's word—and he is wise not to. The King would not go to such lengths to protect the Chevalier. But he would for his brother, and for the stability of the throne."

"You believe Monsieur to be complicit?" I asked.

She shook her head. "I do not know, and we probably never shall. The Duke is a gentle man, but also a weak one, and the Chevalier's influence is strong. The rumours of poison surrounding Minette's death were instant." She paused. "There is a third actor in here, for the King and the Chevalier both want the item hidden and gone. Who might want it to come to light? Condé? The Mancinis? Fouquet? But no—though all have their grievances with the crown, this would not further their causes."

"Who loved the Duchess?" I asked.

"That is a far better question, Toinette."

And then I remembered an overheard conversation between Michel and the English envoy, and how easily he spoke the latter's tongue.

"Her family?" I asked.

Madame stood and kissed me upon the forehead. "You have it, my dear. This tug-of-war over a letter opener stretches between nations. And we can tell none of them." She looked down at the implement still lying on the table. "I have already lied to His Majesty, and said it was destroyed. We cannot let England have it, for that is the sort of proof that could start another war. And yet destroying it would destroy the proof against Lorraine that may be one day needed should the Duke, God forbid, ascend to his brother's throne. It must be kept hidden against such a day."

"But where will you hide it?"

She looked at me sadly. "You will, Toinette, and it is both your peril and your surety."

I picked it up and tucked it into my stays. It slid home like a sword to the scabbard.

§

All seems well for Toinette in Versailles, until Madame disappears again and her Paris house is ransacked. The Shepherdess takes matters into her own hands in Pulp Literature *Issue 35, Summer 2022.*

THE ARTISTS

Herman Lau

Cover artist, Black Tortoise Kowtows

Herman Lau is a freelance artist from Edmonton, Alberta. His interests in illustration stem from the stories and games he grew up with, mythologies full of movement and characters to inspire his drawn illusions. His artwork has been published locally and internationally, including at an exhibition at the Museum of American Illustration in New York and in a collection at State Library Victoria, Australia. He has also run children's visual art programs for non-profit organizations and galleries and provided graphic facilitation services for various municipal groups and initiatives.

The title of the illustration, *Black Tortoise Kowtows,* is from a personal project Herman started called Painted Cards from a Kung Fu Tarot. Herman tells us, "Each card was to represent a technique or concept, and this card was going to be 0 — The Fool. I didn't get far at the time but it's a concept I'd like to revisit. This was the flavour [of the] text I had for it: *kneeling in the mud again? You keep coming back to this place; you are stuck. You will learn a thousand techniques. But the first was how to kneel, to endure. It will cost you. You will revel in the movement, but you will also pay for it the rest of your life. You will miss a call, and never get that chance again. There will be a gift you were always meant to give, something you meant to say, but you will never find the right time. The pain of not moving will outweigh the pain of moving. Strength won't come by mastering the movement, but instead in being mastered by it. Years later, you will misplace the colours of her eyes. It will be winter. You will wake alone and it won't feel so cold. But for now, you're in love with the idea. The question does not become clearer with repetition. But you don't care. Is that why you're——"*

Find more of Herman's work at paintedmonk.wordpress.com, and on Instagram at paintedmonk.

JJ LEE
Artist, end illustration for 'Gumdrop: A Bekker Story'
JJ Lee is best known as a CBC radio personality and an award-nominated memoirist. He is also a talented artist. JJ's cover image, *Ulysses*, for Issue 2, Spring 2014, was a pick of the week by *NewPages* literary review, and we were delighted with the cover he painted for the Issue 7, Summer 2015 feature story by Robert J Sawyer, 'Fallen Angel'. His pulpy, stark, black and white illustrations perfectly embellish his Man in the Long Black Coat stories, and appeared first in Issue 8, Autumn 2015, and again here, with another out-of-this-world print.

HURRICANE NANCY
Illustrator, Cartoon Collection
Nancy was raised in NYC where she marched in union picket lines as a child with her furrier dad, went to the opera and the ballet and symphony concerts with her family, and then discovered Alan Freed concerts and rock and roll … Hail Hail Rock and Roll! Later, in the sixties, she attended The (great) Monterey Pop Festival and Woodstock. Influencing her cartoons as well were many visits to the Museum of Natural History and its great collection of northwest Native American

art. Travelling and working overseas in the early sixties, she fell in love with Hieronymus Bosch. Then, going through the Berlin Wall from the west to the east, she experienced the awakening of how man can make the horror Bosch painted. Coming back from travelling, circa 1965, she settled in NYC on the Lower East Side and soon began producing a cartoon strip for the *East Village Other*. After that, Nancy travelled to the West Coast and kept making cartoons and searching (like going to listen to the Maharishi). In the early seventies, she stopped cartooning when she began helping others get off harmful drugs and better their lives. In 2010, she survived breast cancer and began cartooning again. Nancy has not stopped assisting others or doing cartooning. Fifty pieces of her early work and fifteen of her later work are in the Billy Ireland Cartoon Library and Museum. Learn more at Nancy's website, hurricanenancy.com.

MEL ANASTASIOU
In-house illustrator
Mel Anastasiou loves drawing for *Pulp Literature* because she loves the stories she illustrates. She draws in black and white, working from imagination and inspired by details from Renaissance compositions. You can find illustrations, writing tips, and news about her books and novellas at melanastasiou.wordpress.com, and see more of her artwork on Facebook at Bird and Branch Artwork.

HALL OF FAME

These are the heroes——the Patrons and Pulp Literati whose monthly support helped bring you this issue. Please lift your glasses and give them a rousing cheer!

The Shareholders
Rapscallion

The Brewers
Robin McGillveray
A Bursewicz

The Landlords
Isabel Cushey
Dana Tye Rally

The Innkeepers
Ada Maria Soto
Margot Landels
Ev Bishop
Shannon Saunders
Roger & Anne Anastasiou
Kevin Harris
Gillian Gardiner
Megan Shaw
Susan Jackson
Richard Ohnemus
Nicole Clark

The Cicerones
Elsa Carruthers

The Bartenders
Alana Krider
Richard Gropp

Ron Graves
Kristen Mah
Robert Bose
Victoria McAuley
Dave Wayne
Scott F Gray
Michelle Balfour
Abigail Bruce
Vernice Dietra Malik
Katriona Greenmoor
AD Bane
KT Wagner
Deepthi Atukorala
Margot Spronk
Margaret Elliott
Peter Halasz
Bjarne Hansen
Leny Wagner
Kain Stewart
Chris Olee
kc dyer
Kimberley Aslett
Jan Fagan
Ken Oakes
Brighton Hugg
Alexa Benzaid-Williams
Bryan Moose
Maureen Cooke
Katja Rammer

Kelly Fahy
Mark Catalfano
Norm Rosolen
K Anastasiou
Mike Sylvester
Wichael Tellez

The Regulars
CC Humphreys
Marta Salek
Rina Piccolo
Emily Lonie
Jenny Blackford
Jain Cairns
Akemi Art
BC
Meredith Frazier
Catherine Levinson
Vera
Charity Tahmaseb
Alexander Langer
Marilyn Holt
Risa Wolf
Barbara Pengelly
David Perlmutter
Christine McCullough
Ishbel Newstead
Chad Wilson

If you would like to join the ranks of these worthies, you can become a patron on Patreon at patreon.com/pulplit or join the Pulp Literati through our website at pulpliterature.com/join-pulp-literati/.

COMING SOON FROM PULP LITERATURE PRESS
Allaigna's Song: Chorale
JM LANDELS
THE MAGNIFICENT
FINALE OF THE
BESTSELLING
ALLAIGNA'S SONG
TRILOGY
Allaigna's Song
Overture
JM Landels
Allaigna's Song
Aria
JM Landels
pulpliterature.com

GEIST
go to geist.com/subscribe
or call 1-888-GEIST-EH
Keep it weird.
Subscribe today!
GEIST
BUS STOP NO MORE
LOST CITY
FACT + FICTION • NORTH of AMERICA
NEO-OPSIS
Science Fiction Magazine
www.neo-opsis.ca

on spec
the canadian magazine of the fantastic
Expect the unexpected.
www.onspec.ca

HELP WANTED?

If you are a new writer, or a writer with a
troublesome manuscript,
EVENT's **Reading Service for Writers**
may be just what you need.

Manuscripts will be edited by one of EVENT's editors and receive an
assessment of 700-1000 words, focusing on such aspects of craft as
voice, structure, rhythm and point of view.

eventmagazine.ca

MARKETPLACE

Bookstores

Book Warehouse · 632 Broadway W, Vancouver, BC V5Z 1G1 · 604-872-5711 bookwarehouse.ca

Phoenix On Bowen · 992 Dorman Rd, Bowen Island, BC V0N 1G0 · 604-947-2793

Village Books & Coffee House · 130-12031 First Ave, Richmond, BC V7E 3M1 · 604-272-6601 · villagebooks@shaw.ca

Western Sky Books · 2132-2850 Shaughnessy St, Port Coquitlam, BC V3C 6K5 · 604-461-5602 · store.westernskybooks.com

White Dwarf / Dead Write Books · 3715 10th Ave W, Vancouver, BC V6R 2G5 · 604-228-8223 · whitedwarf@deadwrite.com

Conferences & Events

Word on the Lake · May 2022 · Salmon Arm, BC · wordonthelakewritersfestival.com

When Words Collide · August 2022 Calgary, AB · whenwordscollide.org

Wine Country Writers' Festival · Sept. 2022 · winecountrywriters-festival.ca

Surrey International Writers' Conference October 2022 · siwc.ca

Magazines

Amazing Stories · Back in print! amazingstories.com

The Digest Enthusiast · Digests past & present plus new genre fiction larquepress.com

EVENT Magazine · Poetry & prose eventmagazine.ca

Geist Ideas + Culture · Made in Canada geist.com

Mystery Weekly Magazine The cutting edge of short mystery fiction www.mysteryweekly.com

Neo-opsis · Canadian magazine of science fiction based in Victoria, BC · neo-opsis.ca

OnSpec · The Canadian magazine of the fantastic · onspecmag.wordpress.com

Polar Borealis · Paying market for new Canadian SF&F writers & artists · polarborealis.ca

Room Magazine · Literature, Art & Feminism since 1975 · roommagazine.com

Printing & Publishing

First Choice Books/Victoria Bindery Book printing & binding · graphic design · eBooks · marketing materials 1-800-957-0561 · firstchoicebooks.ca

Writing Resources

Dreamers Creative Writing · Workshops, residencies, contests & more! · www.dreamerswriting.com

Quit the Day Job · A school for writers from Pulp Literature Press pulpliterature.com/quit-the-day-job

The Writers' Lodge on Bowen Island The Muse retreats for writers · pulpliterature.com/calendar-of-events/retreats/

Room Magazine

2022 Contest Calendar

Creative Non-Fiction

1st Prize: $1000 + publication

2nd Prize: $250 + publication

April 1 - June 15

Poetry

1st Prize: $1000 + publication

2nd Prize: $250 + publication

June 15 - August 31

Short Forms

1st Prize: $500 + publication

(two awarded)

September 1 - November 15

Covert Art

1st Prize: $500 + publication

2nd Prize: $50 + publication

November 15 - January 15, 2023

ROOM

Making Space in Literature, Art & Feminism Since 1975

CONTESTS

Pulp Literature runs four annual contests for poetry, flash fiction, and short stories. For contest guidelines, prizes, and entry fees, see pulpliterature.com/contests.

The Hummingbird Flash Fiction Prize
Contest opens: 1 May 2022
Deadline: 15 June 2022
Winner notified: 15 July 2022
Winner published: Issue 37, Winter 2023
Prize: $300

The Raven Short Story Contest
Contest opens: 1 September 2022
Deadline: 15 October 2022
Winner notified: 15 November 2022
Winner published: Issue 38, Spring 2023
Prize: $300

The Bumblebee Flash Fiction Contest
Contest opens: 1 January 2023
Deadline: 15 February 2023
Winner notified: 15 March 2023
Winner published: Issue 39, Summer 2023
Prize: $300

The Magpie Award for Poetry

Contest opens: 1 March 2023

Deadline: 15 April 2023

Winner notified: 15 May 2023

Winner published: Issue 40, Autumn 2023

Prize: $500

$\mathscr{B}$ecome a Patron of Pulp Literature

By supporting *Pulp Literature* on Patreon with $2 or more per month, you will be laying the foundation for a secure future for the magazine, as well as ensuring that you never miss an issue! Your subscription includes four big issues of short stories, novellas, poetry, comics, and novel excerpts, delivered to your door or electronic mailbox each year. **Find us at patreon.com/pulplit**

If you prefer to subscribe through our website, go to pulpliterature. com/subscribe.

Or you can send a cheque with the form below to
Subscriptions, Pulp Literature Press, 21955 16 Ave, Langley BC, V2Z 1K5, Canada

Don't miss an issue!

- ☐ **Send me 2 years (8 issues) at the special rate of $90** (save $30)*
- ☐ **Send me 1 year (4 issues) for $50** (save $10)*
- ☐ **Send me 2 years of digital issues for $30** (save $9.92)
- ☐ **Send me 1 year of digital issues for $17.50** (save $2.47)

Name: ____

Address: ____

City: _______________________________ Prov. / State: _________

Postal code: _____________ Country:_____________________

Email: ____

- ☐ Payment enclosed
- ☐ Bill me
- ☐ New
- ☐ Renewal

Make cheques payable in Canadian funds to Pulp Literature Press. Include email address for digital editions and Paypal billing, or subscribe at www.pulpliterature.com.

*for postage outside Canada add $20 per year in North America or $36 per year overseas.